A Walk in the Park

A Novel

Dianne Zimmermann

Publishing Assistance
BookCrafters, Parker, Colorado.
www.BookCrafters.net

*I dedicate this book to my friends
whose never-ending encouragement
drove me on when the going got tough.*

Acknowledgements

I wish to thank my friends for all their interest and encouragement in all my writing endeavors. *A Walk in the Park* is my seventh book. I wish to express special thanks to my friends Lou Platten and LA Mott for their years of encouragement, ideas, proofreading, and editing skills.

Chapter One

"Come on Emma, it's time for your walk," said Laura, "go get your leash." Of course, Emma did not. Even after Laura had lowered the peg so Emma could reach her leash, she did not retrieve it. Emma was very smart, but so far she had not caught on to the new trick yet. She just looked up at Laura as if to say, "I'm not a retriever, you'll have to get it for me, and don't forget the poop bags." Laura did have a history of forgetting them, and that was why all her jackets and pants pockets had plastic grocery store bags stuffed in them now. Laura retrieved the leash but made a mental note to remind herself to work on helping Emma with her retrieval skills.

Emma and Laura lived in a condo across the street from Forest Park in St. Louis. Laura loved her condo location, so convenient for a walk in the park, just a crosswalk away. So their daily routine consisted of crossing Skinker Blvd. at the crosswalk and walking the paved path in Forest Park. They did this at least once a day every day, sometimes twice a day. Laura loved getting out into nature. She loved walking and riding her bike on the six-mile paved path throughout and circumventing the park.

She was proud of Forest Park. To Laura's best recollection, she thought Forest Park consisted of thirty-six hundred acres and was over five-hundred acres larger than Central Park in New York City. The 1902 St. Louis World's Fair was held in Forest Park and introduced the world to the ice cream cone. The World's Fair Pavilion still stands up the hill from the Boathouse Restaurant in the center of the park just north of the wZrld-famous free admission St. Louis Zoo.

Laura and her late husband, Hank, used to play golf in the park's three wonderful golf courses. There is a large lake in the park and a place adjacent to the Boathouse Restaurant where paddle boats and kayaks can be rented for a leisurely paddle around the lake. After a paddle around the lake, you can sit out on the patio and have a nice lunch or dinner at the Boathouse Restaurant that overlooks the lake. Laura and Hank enjoyed many memorable outdoor patio dinners at the Boathouse before walking over to enjoy performances at the St. Louis Muny outdoor theatre. They were season ticket holders and enjoyed many performances there.

Long before Laura's husband Hank was even thinking about retiring, they downsized and sold their home in neighboring Ladue and moved into their condo on Skinker Boulevard, across from the park. Another one of their favorite things to do in mid-June was to attend the free Shakespeare in the Park Festival on Art Hill. They would pack a picnic basket with a bottle of wine and sit on a blanket and enjoy the performances. They also loved the frequent concerts held in the park.

One year in particular was most joyful was when the grandstand at the Arch grounds on the Mississippi River was being renovated, so the July 4th fireworks display and summer concert series was moved from below the Gateway Arch and held in Forest Park above the lake on breezy Art Hill. Laura and Hank's most favorite free summer concert in the park was the Fourth of July celebration with a Melissa Etheridge concert. It was right after she came out with her latest Memphis Blues album. It was a nice warm evening, and the park was rocking with rhythm, and the ice-cold Summer Shady orange flavored beer went down brisk and refreshing. It was the perfect setting for sitting on a blanket on a grassy hillside with a picnic basket dinner and in the cool breeze of the evening on Art Hill. Legend has it that in years past, during unseasonably hot summers when no one had home air conditioning, folks would spend warm summer nights camped out and sleeping on breezy Art Hill.

Laura and Hank enjoyed the concerts, Shakespeare Festival in the Park plays, and the Art and History museums. They enjoyed so many events in the park, it was their favorite place. Those joyful park moments ended abruptly for Hank when he became ill with dementia. Seems it came on fast, and then everything slowed to a halt very quickly. The disease progressed rapidly, and a regimen of medicinal treatments and therapies did not seem to help. Hank's dementia was slow to come at first, he would forget little things I told him. He would forget his keys, or where he put them. The constant searches, all thought of as just a part of getting older. But Laura worried, for she found his keys in the refrigerator. She saw that his condition kept getting worse. It was so difficult to watch his health decline, especially when he was so alert and active all his life. Hank had been a detective on the St. Louis city police force for many years. He loved his job, and he was good at his job.

Before Hank became ill, he would come home from work and discuss his cases with Laura. He worked on missing persons cases, the missing wife, the kidnapped child, things like that. Laura was drawn in by the mystery and suspense of it all, so she would sometimes help him try to figure out scenarios and clues. She tried to help him connect the dots and make sense of it all. Sometimes there was no rhyme or reason why people did the things they did.

Hank and Laura came to realize that most crimes are committed out of the impulse of rage or in the spur of an angry moment without thinking about the consequences. Laura was interested in crime work and very helpful to Hank, not only because she was interested in the work, but she discovered that she had a slight edge, she had the gift of being very knowing and psychic. She had a very intuitive nature about herself. She could sense things. She discovered her gifts in her mid-forties while engaging in conversation with a friend.

She had lunch one day with her friend and fellow running buddy, Judy. They were having a casual conversation at lunch about which brand of shoes were the better running shoes, when out of the blue, Laura sensed that Judy had breast cancer in her right breast. It was as if the energy she sensed was coming from the cancer. While listening to her friend talk about the different styles of running shoes, suddenly the knowing, intuitive thought that her friend had cancer popped into Laura's head. The thought left, then a few minutes later, as they were talking about their grown kids not giving them grandchildren, the thought came back. She pushed the thought away again. But after a few minutes, the thought returned. Finally, while they were finishing their soup and sandwiches, she asked her friend how she had been feeling lately.

"Well, a little out of sorts, I guess," sighed Judy. "I have a doctor's appointment tomorrow."

"Would you like me to go with you?" Laura found herself casually offering.

Judy thought it was nice of her to ask, but for a second, she wondered why it seemed Laura was concerned. Laura did not want to worry her friend and hoped Judy did not sense her concern but thought she just being polite. Of course at the time, Judy did not know that Laura was psychic, Laura never told anyone that she sometimes got senses of knowing. It came out of the blue.

She couldn't explain it, so she never brought it up. Sometimes when she and Hank would drive somewhere, she would suggest another route in order to avoid heavy traffic or an incident or accident ahead that would only detain them. Through the years, Hank had learned to rely on Laura's "good judgement." He often referred to life with all-knowing Laura as "just a walk in the park."

"That's sweet of you to offer to come with me, thanks," Judy said. "I would like that, and we can have lunch afterward."

Laura was glad she went with her friend that time, because the lab found something in her blood test results indicating she did indeed have breast cancer. But it was in the early stages, so a good prognosis was hopeful. Thankfully years later her friend, Judy, was still doing well.

Chapter Two

Laura was lonely and missed Hank after he passed. So one year in early spring, she decided to get a dog from the humane society. She immediately bonded with the approximately five-year-old Rottweiler, she named Emma. Emma was already wonderfully trained, and they loved to go for walks around the neighborhood and in the park. Springtime was always a wonderful time in the park. The flowers were blooming, birds were singing, and baby animals were being born. Sometimes after their walks, Laura would ride her bike around the neighborhood and the six-mile trail around the park.

One day Laura rode her road-bike on Wydown Avenue and stopped at the traffic light at the intersection, then crossed Skinker Boulevard into Forest Park. As soon as she rode into the park, she saw cars were stopped ahead of her. She rode her bike alongside of them to see what the hold-up was. And that was when she spotted a mother duck leading her family of little ducklings across the street. The drivers stopped in both directions to watch and allow the mother duck and her family of little ones to safely cross to the other side. Mama duck had seven little ones following her across the street, heading toward the lake. But there was an obstacle for the little baby ducks to tackle, a curb. Laura stopped alongside the cars and watched the duck family cross the street, so sweet to watch. But to her aching heart, she watched as the last little baby duck, evidently the smallest one, could not make it up the curb. It struggled hopelessly. The poor little thing looked frantic in fear of being left behind. Laura's heart was breaking for the poor little thing. There was another bicyclist just up ahead who had also stopped to watch the commotion. Suddenly Laura found herself pleading with the woman to help her.

"Come on, we have to help it," cried Laura to the other bicyclist. So they both laid their bikes down against the curb and ran over to help the little struggling baby duck. Unfortunately, Laura drove the frantic little duck back into the street in front of the, thankfully, still stopped cars. The drivers were now entertained watching the two ladies run around in circles trying to guide the frantic baby duck back toward the curb as they tried to catch it in their hands. Mother duck never turned around, she and the rest of the family were already in the grass only a few yards away from the edge of the lake.

Mama duck with the rest following her had no idea they had left one baby duck behind. They were oblivious and slowly waddled on toward the lake. Laura just knew that It had to be a funny sight for the stopped motorists to watch as these two women practically running into each other, darted back and forth trying to corral and catch the little duck who was not having any of it.

Finally, the other lady caught the baby duck when it went under her bicycle lying against the curb. She gently cupped it in her hands and carefully carried it over to the edge of the lake and gently set it in the water. Laura watched feeling like an out-of-breath failure. When the woman gently set the little baby duck on the water, mother duck turned and looked, she looked as if she was surprised that she had lost one of her babies. She immediately swam over to the little one as did all the other little baby ducks. Little baby duck was back in the fold again.

"Well, that was fun and exciting," exclaimed Laura still out of breath as was the other woman.

"Just a walk in the park," the woman managed to speak but still out of breath.

"For sure," sighed Laura taking deep breaths. She found it refreshing to hear the saying Hank always said, "just a walk in the park." It made her smile. She immediately liked this woman.

"Hi, my name is Ellen," offered the fellow bicyclist, who was dressed in helmet, sunglasses, bike gloves and biking jersey and pants just as Laura was dressed.

"Hi, my name is Laura," she smiled, "so nice to meet you. Thank you for helping me with the little duck. It was so painful to watch the poor little thing struggle, being left behind like that, trying to get up the curb without any help."

"Oh, I was only too happy to help," Ellen answered. The poor little thing was breaking my heart too."

Both ladies were still a little out of breath, both now back at the curb reaching for their water bottles on the bikes.

"I see a bench right over there, want to sit and rest a bit?" asked Ellen sensing that they clicked somehow, and she very badly in need of someone to talk to.

Laura was all too glad to sit and rest and perhaps meet a new friend. So they walked their bikes over to the bench under a huge oak tree surrounded with flowers and bushes.

"Looks like you ride a lot too," commented Laura. Ellen had a road bike like Laura. Laura being an avid bicyclist was quick to notice the slender figure, firm upper arms, flat stomach and strong legs of a fellow dedicated bicyclist.

"Yes, I do. Personally, I find it is great therapy," commented Ellen, "My husband and I had been having a rough time of it. We've not getting along very well."

"Oh, I'm sorry to hear that," Laura was sympathetic. Of course, being psychic, Laura got an intuitive hint of Ellen's sorrow when Ellen removed her helmet and sunglasses and she saw the sadness in her eyes. It was most evident that Ellen was troubled.

"It is not good; he has threatened to beat the crap out of me if I try to leave him." Ellen said with tears in her eyes. Ellen got right to it. She desperately needed to vent. She did not know where to turn for help as she was afraid of her husband. He was so possessive, demanding to know her every move.

Just then Laura's psychic juices fired up and she got an uneasy feeling in her stomach. Something was not right. She felt this woman was truly in danger.

"What's your husband's name?" Laura asked.

"It's Mark, Mark Dotson," Ellen replied with a sad voice.

"Have you been married long?"

"About twenty-seven years, we have a grown son."

For some strange reason, Laura had the feeling they needed to get out of the park right away, she was becoming ever more uneasy.

"Hey, Ellen," said Laura, "would you like ride over to my place? I just live a short way up the hill and across the street, and I have cold lemonade and iced tea at home."

"Oh, you live in one of the condos on Skinker Boulevard near Clayton Road?" asked Ellen. "I have always wanted to see those. There was a time when I thought about looking for a place to rent over there."

Laura was happy to hear that Ellen wanted to leave and got up quickly from the bench taking a step toward her bike. She still had that uneasy feeling and wanted to get out of the park with Ellen. Ellen seemed like a nice, sweet person and she wanted to help her.

"Ah crap, there he is," sighed Ellen frozen in place with fright.

"Where?" asked Laura.

"In the big red Ford pickup truck coming this way," Ellen said in a shaky voice.

"Oh, oh," sighed Laura, she could see that the man was looking around as he drove very slowly, as if looking for something or someone. Laura suspected he was searching for Ellen. The two women were close to big bushes, so as they saw her husband look in the other direction, they quickly ran with their bikes to hide in the bushes where they stood quietly.

"Let's wait a bit," suggested Ellen. While they waited, hoping Mark would leave the area, they quickly added each other to their phone contact information.

Then they quickly put their sunglasses and helmets back on.

"Sorry about my husband," Ellen apologized. "Since he got fired from the oil refinery job he had for years, he has been a mess. Now he is trying his hand at construction work. He got fired because he and his boss did not get along. I found out recently he has been fired in the past from other jobs as well. I think he has a problem working for people. This must be his lunch time if he is driving through the park."

"That's too bad about your marriage," offered Laura, "just know if you ever need to, you can come and stay with me. He doesn't know me or where I live, so you would be safe. Laura felt sorry for Ellen, she could see that she was visibly shaken.

"I think he's gone now," Ellen thought and hoped so anyway. It had been at least twenty minutes and as antsy and impatient as Mark was, and has always been, she figured he gave up searching for her and left the park.

They were about to come out from behind the big bushes when suddenly, in a flurry of sounds of snapping twigs and forced to the side leafy branches, a large man came bursting through and rushed up to Ellen. She screamed. He was tall, a big guy, unshaven with long shaggy hair and a totally unkept appearance. He came out of nowhere. The man was angry, and with his big hand he slapped Ellen face hard. Laura reflectively slipped in closer between the branches of the bush. Lucky for Ellen he mostly missed her face and hit her helmet knocking her sunglasses crooked. Before she could react, in the next second, he angrily grabbed her under her arm with one hand, and grabbed her bike with the other, dragging both her and her bicycle toward the street where his truck was parked. Ellen was cursing and kicking, trying to break free from his grasp.

Laura stood and watched in horror. He had paid no attention to Laura, acted like he did not see her. His temper and evil focus were solely on Ellen. Laura heard her crying as her husband dragged her off, it frightened her. She was worried for her. He moved fast and in seconds, they had reached the truck. Laura watched in horror as he literally threw her bike in the bed of the pickup truck and almost simultaneously opened the driver side door and shoved her in and swiftly climbed in behind her. Laura was so frightened for her. She did not know what to do. The big red truck sped away leaving behind a cloud of thick gray diesel exhaust. The smell of oil lingered in the air as a troubled and shook-up Laura rode her bike through it on her way back to the safety of her home.

When Laura got home, she hugged Emma. She was so shaken about what she had just witnessed, and Emma was a comfort to her. What could she do? Her only hope was that maybe Ellen could escape him somehow at some point. Laura was afraid to call Ellen in case her husband would see that she was trying to contact her. Laura wanted to remain unknown to Mark. She wanted that so Ellen could, if she ever got the chance to get away from him, come hide at her condo. Laura would be only too happy to help her. It was slightly personal to Laura because her first marriage was to a hellhole man like Mark, so she could easily sympathize with Ellen.

Days passed and Laura wondered how Ellen was doing. She hoped that she was well and doing okay. Her husband looked mighty angry when he carried her over to the truck and opened the driver side door, shoved her in and sped off. Laura was curious and decided to go for a bike ride toward the area where Ellen lived which was just west of her own neighborhood.

Laura decided she would ride her bike through the neighborhood behind her condo and head west over to De Mun Avenue where Ellen and Mark's house was located. Laura was glad that she had quickly traded contact information with Ellen as they hid behind the bushes. She had Ellen's street address, email address, and cell phone number information, but she was afraid

14

to contact her. Ellen had said her husband was very possessive, controlling, and wanted to know her every move at all times, so Laura was afraid to try to reach her for fear of putting Ellen in further danger.

The De Mun Avenue area was a quaint neighborhood with small shops and restaurants and Kaldi's, a popular coffee house. Laura rode her bike around the area for a while, up and down the many one-way streets. She did not see Ellen's husband's big red pickup truck parked anywhere near their house. There was a small park across the street from the coffee shop, Laura thought she would get a bite and a cup of java and either sit outside on their patio or walk across the street to the small park and sit on a bench. She parked her bike at the bike rack with the other bikes and went inside. She looked around as she entered. It was a rather small place in an old building as were all the buildings in that area. In the back room she saw there were open tables available; that is, if she decided to stay inside with her coffee and pastry. As her eyes adjusted from sunny daylight to the dimness of the room, she slowly scanned the area. In the corner near the window, she noticed a woman with long dark hair sitting at a table busy working on her laptop. Was it Ellen? Laura was not quite sure if it was Ellen, sitting alone appearing to be concentrating on what she was typing.

"Ellen, is that you?" Laura asked with a quiet voice, and she took a few steps closer. She stood a table's distance away waiting for the woman to look up. Finally the woman raised her head and looked around.

"Laura?" Ellen shyly smiled when she looked up. Her hair was long and hung down with long strands around her face. Laura took a step closer. In the sunlight streaming in from the window, she could see the dark area around Ellen's left eye. It was black and blue and there was a small cut.

"Are you okay?" asked Laura, "I have been worried about you. I was hoping you would call or text me."

"I was afraid to contact you because Mark checks my phone all the time. He censors my calls," complained Ellen in a sad voice. She went on to explain. "There are only a couple of people that I am allowed to communicate with. I come here most days for the WiFi. Today I am journaling, Mark thinks it's stupid. I say I am coming here to journal, and I do; but I also come here to secretly apply for jobs online. I thought I would apply at the new Amazon Distribution Center that just opened up in Fenton."

"Oh cool, I hope you get the job," Laura said with encouragement, "that would be great." Laura was glad to see that Ellen was taking measures to break out of her abusive marriage, her physical and mental prison, and do something good for herself.

"Ouch," moaned Ellen lightly touching her face, "the jerk hit me. I'm so tired of being his punching bag."

"Your eye looks sore. Is there anything I can do to help?" asked Laura feeling sorry for Ellen. Ellen raised her hand up to touch the area again. She slightly patted the area around her left eye and found it still felt swollen. Laura noticed Ellen had tears in her eyes. And her heart went out to her. Laura could sympathize, as she recalled those horrid days with her first husband who was so abusive.

"It's getting better, thanks for asking," Ellen's hand was shaking a bit when she touched the area as if the pain around her eye had permeated throughout her whole physical and emotional being. She was only too glad that she found a friend in Laura.

"So, is your husband at work now?" asked Laura. She remembered Ellen told her that her husband was a construction worker.

"I guess," grimaced Ellen, "it is where he is supposed to be anyway. I have no idea how much he makes; he never tells me anything. I get an allowance that includes money for buying groceries. He doesn't want me to work."

"Well, if there is anything I can do to help you, you will let me know, okay?" offered Laura, as Ellen reached over and pulled out a chair and motioned for Laura to sit at her table.

"Would you help me kill him and dispose of the body?" Ellen asked matter-of-factly, looking at Laura without blinking an eye.

"Hm, you are kidding me, right?" Laura asked feeling a little worried about what Ellen just said. And wishing she would not have said it, because you never know when you can be subpoenaed to testify in a court of law.

"No, not really," sighed Ellen, "but, come on people are murdered every day, and people get away with it."

Hearing Ellen say that did not ease Laura's feelings any about what she was hearing.

"I'm not sure that is true. In fact, I know it is not true as my husband was a police detective for years," explained Laura. "He was a pretty good one at that. I used to help him with his cases, just for kicks, and because I was very interested. So many evenings he would come home scratching his head trying to figure out a case, and I would help him go through the evidence and case files. He always told me that I was the most intuitive and psychic detective he knew. That I just knew things. So many times, it did come in handy, I would tell him where to look, or who to suspect, or where to take another look. One time, I even told him, correctly, mind you, where I thought the body was buried. And at one point, his department hired me for a particular case involving a missing child." Laura was proud of her accomplishments.

"Did you find the child?" Ellen asked about the case.

"Yes, I directed them right to her shallow grave in the woods. Her father was the guilty one in that case. After the shallow grave was discovered, he broke down and confessed to all the sub-human atrocities he committed with the girl, his very own daughter. He was abusing her for years, and finally she had enough and hit him with a cast iron skillet filled with scrambled eggs she was cooking for his breakfast. This angered him, and he yanked the skillet out of her hands and beat her to death with it. Then he had the audacity to say that he missed her."

"That's awful," Ellen said sadly.

"Would you say every time he gets mad and hits you his punches get more vicious and brutal?" asked Laura.

"Yes, I guess, I would say that," sighed Ellen. "He kicked me in the stomach too last night, and I still hurt." Ellen looked very sad.

"We need to get you away from him, don't you think?" asked Laura.

"But I'm afraid. He said he would hunt me down and kill me if I leave him."

"The way things are going, with his abuse becoming more violent, is a pure sign that over time, he is likely to kill you anyway," stated Laura matter-of-factly, "Studies show that spousal abuse gets worse over time until the abuser ends up killing the victim; that is, if she continues to stay with him."

"I know," sighed Ellen, "I have heard.,"

"Have you ever called the police on him, like for a domestic dispute?"

"I did one time, then chickened out when the police arrived and told them that everything was okay. I explained to the officers it was just a misunderstanding, and he apologized and promised to treat me better, and we were getting counseling. The whole time I was speaking with the officers at the front door, Mark stood quietly behind me. He did not say much to the police, and I was afraid to, because he had a knife at my back when I spoke with the officers. I could feel it, and I was frightened. I was even more afraid when I saw the officers turn to leave. Because I feared that when they drove away, I was really going to get it, and I did. He beat me very badly after they left."

"That is horrible" Laura could not believe what she was hearing. "That was awful; no one should have to go through such torment and fear. "

"I have to go now, I have to be back home by three o'clock when he gets off work," revealed Ellen with tears in her eyes and a shaky voice.

"Okay, then," said Laura feeling helpless. She wanted to help this poor woman.

"Try to come here again tomorrow, same time, okay Laura?" asked Ellen really needing a friend to talk to. Mark would not let her see any of her friends. Ellen guessed by now they were former friends since she had cut off all contact with them to adhere to Mark's threats.

"Sure, I'll be here," Laura smiled. She saw the tears well up in Ellen's swollen eyes. This poor woman Laura thought. No one should have to live in fear like that.

Chapter Three

As Laura rode her bike through the quiet neighborhood streets back to her condo, she wondered how she could help Ellen. She missed detective work and those crime solving days when she helped Hank solve cases. She thought about what Ellen had said and wondered how it would be to plan a crime. Through the years when she helped her husband, she always saw the way that the crime could have been successful and prevented detection. It was just her personality to see both sides of a situation.

Sometimes she even found herself rooting for the perpetrator, especially if they were escaping an abusive situation. But most of the time, she saw that people let things build up and then reacted in the moment of a heighten emotional state without thinking, usually using angry impulsive measures. And that acting out of impulse always left distinctive clues, sometimes very creative alibis gave them away. Often she felt if the perpetrator were not impulsive, but rather preplanned a bit and thought about an actions' consequences ahead of time, they actually could have taken certain precautions that would have allowed them to get away with their crime. For example, take more time to plan it to make it look like an accident. Laura was a bit of an Agatha Christy in reverse, she moved from solving crime, to figuring out how they could have been done better without getting caught. Laura had a great idea: what if a crime was set up in two ways, one way for the detective to solve it as a curious accident or as a mysterious unsolvable case, as a way to fulfill the deed? Her mind was spinning with ideas. She had all kinds of questions for Ellen when she met up with her the next day.

She was home now and put her bike away, Emma, her sweet Rottweiler, was eagerly awaiting her return as she sat, so proud of herself, with her leash in her mouth waiting patiently at the door.

Chapter Four

"Well, aren't you something, getting your leash form the hook all by yourself like I showed you," smiled Laura. Laura hugged the big ninety-eight pound, solid but very gentle, Rottweiler.

"Okay come on then, let's go for your walk, just give me a minute to change my clothes." She quickly changed out of her biking jersey and riding shorts into sweats as Emma watched and waited patiently. In five minutes, they were out the door.

It had been a beautiful day and an evening walk in the park would be wonderful. Laura loved the sights and sounds of nature as the birds sang praise in their last songs of the day. They walked the park path further up the hill on Skinker Boulevard and continued east on the path that led through a grove of tall pine trees. Laura could feel the energy of the wonderfully scented tall pines. She liked to gently touch the pine needle branches and ground herself. She bought a grounding tester from Earthing.com and found that just touching the stem of the leaves of a tree for a minute or two, left her grounded for about two hours. All shoes are made with rubber soles these days, and leather soles which would ground you on grass or concrete are practically obsolete. Most days she walked barefoot in the grass in her condo complex yard. She was big on Earthing now for balancing her chakras and body's electrical system. We are electric, she had read about that and read multiple testimonies of grounding healing stories.

She also watched the "Healing" documentaries on the GAIA Network. When Laura grew tired of watching the cable news channels, she switched to GAIA and watched documentaries and interviews of people's healing and spiritual experiences. The Earthing experience caught her attention, and it was easy and simple to do, just walk barefoot on concrete or in the grass, or hold onto branches on trees or bushes with both hands for a minute or two. She bought the Earthing mat strip, the book entitled, *Earthing*, and an outlet ground tester came with it. She laid on the grounded mat every night and in the morning tested herself by holding a battery operated testing device, and if the green light stayed on, you were grounded, as she was, each morning. She found that she slept better, had so much more energy, less aches and pains, and she found that she could even think more clearly. And Earthing was free, all you had to do was touch the stems of leaves, or walk barefoot in the grass or on concrete.

Learning all of this made her think of her childhood on the farm, when as a bit of a tomboy she played in the dirt with her trucks and cars, helped in the garden, walked behind the push mower and mowed the lawn, ate their own farm raised beef, chicken and eggs, and vegetables from the garden. No wonder she was a healthy kid. Laura had always led a healthy lifestyle, so she loved getting older, because along with age comes more knowledge and wisdom. Laura believed that we are spiritual beings here on Earth to experience life in human form. She also believed we each have guides and archangels that come with us to help with our assignment we give ourselves for this lifetime.

Laura believed there was no need for illness just because you were getting older. Laura thought illness need not be part of the natural order. She learned that our emotions and thoughts control and create our health conditions. That it is necessary to release stress along with good exercise and eating organically. It is why she liked to ride her road bike, it gave her a full body workout, especially when her hands were on the drop handlebars while climbing hills. She felt the benefits to her whole body and overall health with each pull of her hands and arms and pull and push of her legs as her feet are clipped into her biking cleats. She loved hill climbing and the pull on her inner arms and inner thighs, and her stomach and abdomen. It is a full body workout happening all at the same time. The only other form of exercise she especially loved was walking in the park with Emma as it was good exercise for Emma too.

Laura was deep in thought as she and Emma walked the paved path that meandered through the woods and near the perimeter of the park. They passed family groups gathering for outside cookouts. She observed people sitting at picnic tables under the canopy of the huge oak trees that filled the park. She could have walked further but Emma wasn't a pup anymore, she was getting up there in age. So they turned around and headed back for home. Emma was ready to go back home too as she was finished with doing her business and snooping all her favorite spots along the path.

Emma ate and laid down on her own grounding mat to take a nap while Laura sat down and made notes of some possibilities of successful crime scenarios. Grounding gave Laura lots of energy, sometimes she would wake up in the middle of the night and read, or watch *Date Line*. She was amazed that some crimes were committed in the heat of passion, in the spur of the moment, while others were well-planned in advance, like death by ocean cruise in foreign waters, or poisoning death by antifreeze in beer. Or as one woman did, used large quantities of clear eye solution in her husband's water and beer which restricted capillaries in his chest that led to his death.

Through Laura's dedicated hours of research, she found that the biggest factor was that most crimes were crimes of passion, some premeditated and planned out scientifically; but, then only to go awry in the heat of a moment. Laura found the human psyche fascinating and had read many books on the subject. Most people would not think of watching a crime television show are reading a murder mystery at bedtime, for fear of nightmares, but it was Laura's preferred way of getting sleepy and falling to sleep. And sleep she did, without nightmares, but rather dreaming about seeing Ellen at the coffee shop again the next day.

Chapter Five

"Hi Ellen, good to see you," Laura said with cheese Danish and large coffee in hand for them both. She stepped closer to the table, carefully looking over Ellen, hoping not to see new injuries and evidence of more abuse from her husband.

"Hi, come sit," Ellen smiled as she pulled out a chair for Laura to sit and join her at the table. She had been there for a while already sipping coffee and working on her laptop.

As Laura settled in her chair, she continued to observe Ellen hoping not to see any more signs of bruises and cuts. Ellen caught on to Laura's visual examination and had to make a comment.

"You do know that some men injure you where injuries cannot be so easily detected," noted Ellen. She realized that Laura was checking her over and in her own way appreciated her concern.

"You also need to be careful about internal injuries." warned Laura, "is your stomach still hurting?"

"My stomach is better, much better," revealed Ellen. "I just wish that I could figure out a way to leave him without him killing me in the process."

"Kill him first," Laura found herself saying out loud, surprising herself at her boldness sounding like Ellen did the day before. At that moment she finally realized that she indeed watched too many crime shows such as *Date Line* and *Unsolved Mysteries*.

Laura could not believe she said what she said--and out loud. She put the thought out there and thoughts can become reality, *what was she getting herself in to*, she wondered. Laura was getting worked up, and tired of people being over run and abused in relationships. Seems the strongest personality rules while the other partner is treated like property without any say or freedom to be themselves. Laura had some ideas to pass by Ellen.

Laura had just spent half the night coming up with disappearing husband ideas and possible spousal demise plans. She had questions for Ellen about her husband's routines and habits. A devised plan would have to be the perfect crime, Laura had been studying crimes for years and she knew the perfect crime was possible.

"What?" asked Ellen with huge eyes filled with awe. She leaned in closer so neighboring occupied tables could not catch the drift of their conversation.

"Does your husband have a life insurance policy?" asked Laura.

"He doesn't share a lot with me, but this I do know.

Yes, he does have benefits through his construction work, why?"

"How is his health?" Laura asked in a soft voice, more of a whisper, and with a curious tone to her voice. She kept her voice low as she was concerned that neighboring tables could overhear what she was saying.

"Well, he drinks more than he eats. He's a beer drinker and he is overweight. He eats junk food by the ton. As a matter of fact, junk food is all he eats, now that I think about it," shared Ellen.

"I see," commented Laura, "anything else?"

"Seems he never likes what I cook, I have no idea why he demands I have dinner on the table when he gets home from work, because he usually complains about what I cook. Nothing is ever good enough. He acts like it would kill him to pay me a polite compliment and a give me nice thank you once in a while. It is like he has to keep me down, and my spirit broken."

"My guess would be that he is terrified of you leaving him," stated Laura.

"Well, he sure has a funny way of showing it," Ellen replied in a doubtful tone.

"He is afraid that if he compliments you, it will build your confidence in yourself, and you'll get a big head, and that you may then just want to leave his sorry ass," Laura explained.

"What?" It was the first time Ellen was actually seeing the strange emotional weaknesses in Mark.

"His grasp is so tight, that he would rather see you dead than you leave him," continued Laura.

"I have got to get away from that crazy lunatic," sighed Ellen. She had clearly had enough.

"Well, if you wait long enough, seems those bad unhealthy habits should do him in. But be forewarned that his anger will only get worse as his heath deteriorates and he feels like hell. So be careful, you may not outlast him if he keeps abusing you more severely on a regular basis. A serious internal injury could take you down."

"Can't I just run him over in the driveway with his own truck?" asked Ellen, she was coming to her wits' end. The marriage was horrible and it's over. Actually, it had been over for years.

"Sure, if you can make it count and finish the deed by running over him only once, then and only then, can it look like an accident. Where women get into trouble, is they are so angry, their anger overtakes them, and they run over their abusive husbands. They are so mad at them, they then back up over him again, or turn around and run over him again, sometimes, again and again. That is not wise behavior, and that obvious brutal vicious behavior will get you the go-directly-to-jail card," advised Laura.

"Wish he would just disappear into thin air," sighed Ellen sounding more depressed than usual. "But then I guess I need the body to collect the insurance money, really don't even want it, it's not worth it, I just want him out of my life."

"I know it's tough," sympathized Laura.

"Sometimes I envision him so drunk that he falls out

of the truck and gets run over by those stupid dual rear wheels with the naked lady mud flaps."

"That would certainly be a convenient accident," acknowledged Laura.

"He punches me all the time, yet I can't retaliate without going to jail," realized Ellen, "it's not fair."

"What upsets me," exclaimed Laura, "is that he gets away with punching you, and kicking you, and whatever. He has you so scared. It is exactly how he wants you to be, so you will never leave him. You are being brutalized because of his big-baby fear of being left all alone. It is as if he hates the realization that he is truly dependent on you, as if you are his mother. He hates that he feels that way and blames you for it." Laura was tapping into her amateur psychological analytic toolbox at that moment.

"What do you mean?" asked Ellen.

"He's the big baby here, certainly not a real man in my eyes. Now, my husband, Hank, was a true gentleman," commented Laura. "But let's say you have had just enough and you lose it and shoot him, then you are guilty of murder. Nothing he has done to you in the past will matter. The courts do not see years of abuse factoring into you shooting him in self-defense one day. White men patriarchal rule sets the stage, and they set the stage and the rules up to suit themselves. He is a privileged white man, and you are a woman, a second-class citizen in a patriarchal society. This is nothing new, it's been going on for hundreds if not thousands of years. You do realize we live in a very patriarchal white supremacist society; a patriarchal society where social norms are dictated by reptilian brained males who lack a sense of consciousness and only want to conquer and control the masses. And these males are into religion, banking, healthcare, big drug and chemical corporations, and our brain-washed socially-engineered government leaders. They are aiming toward the striping of the freedoms of democracy, taking us into a one-party totality dictatorship following dumbing down and depopulation tactics. And it would be just your luck you would probably get a very conservative misogynist white male judge on the bench to rule your case. In my own humble opinion, women are victims who are screwed over time and time again, period."

"I know that there are good men out there," remarked Ellen, "somewhere."

"My husband, Hank, was a good man," claimed Laura, "He was a dedicated detective till his dying day, and he always said, women have never been equal in the white man's eyes. Instead, all women are grouped by white men with the other non-white races they think are lessor beings. Women are put into the minority group by patriarchal rule, and this is just a known fact. For some reason, it is just natural for white men to believe they are the chosen Arian race privileged ones, with self-proclaimed declared royalty and authority status. It all stems from the Roman Empire and then the British Empire; royalty rules over women and minorities, like it or not," explained Laura.

"Why is that, Laura?" asked Ellen.

"Okay, I can give you a quick history lesson summary, I think," said Laura. "Here is the way I learned it as I read *Alien World Order*, by Len Kasten. Seems not very nice Reptilians were the first on Earth. these Reptilians are without conscience. They only want to install fear, conquer and overtake. They originated from the Draco constellation, then went to Orion constellation where their women were tired of doing all the heavy work for the males. So, the women rose up and the queen took over the king's rule and dominated the males. The Reptilians ended up on the island of Lemuria, and humans from Lyra ended up on the island of Atlantis. The Reptilians on Lemuria aggravated the humans on Atlantis, and the Atlantans with their superior weapons forced the Reptilians underground. The Reptilians lacked weapons to fight back, so they infiltrated the human psychic via the dream state and created Reptilian/Human Hybrids. And there you have it, that is how certain powerful evil Reptilians managed to get into ruling positions. It is because they are Reptilian, without a soul or consciousness. They have no love in their heart as other pure human beings do. And the Reptilian Hybrids hold a grudge against women, as they have not forgotten how the women over ran them on Orion, it's payback time.

"That does makes sense why most men in power seem self-serving and evil," said Ellen. "I sure see it in my husband. He must be one of the left-over evil ones."

"Well, evidently that old patriarchal rule will end one day as more and more minorities and women are going for the powerful positions in corporate and in the political arena," suggested Laura.

"I don't think running for office will help me," Ellen said with tears of desperation brimming in her eyes. "I just don't know what to do anymore."

"Well, you said his health wasn't good, he is drunk all the time, so he could he be accident prone too. You know, being overweight, and drunk, could cause you to be a little off balance."

"Like maybe he could lose his balance at the top of the basement steps," wondered Ellen out loud. "We have stairs to the second floor, too."

"Yeah, well, you never know," sighed Laura speaking in a lowered voice.

"Last night he came home really drunk, he picked a fight with me as I was coming out of our upstairs bathroom. He backed me up against the wall in the hall near the steps. I was so afraid. One good shove, and I would have been flying down the steps."

"Hm, too bad he didn't go flying down the steps," proclaimed Laura in a sense of wishful thinking.

"Has your husband ever been in trouble with the law?" asked Laura. She was mainly just curious but assumed someone with such an ill spirited temper most likely has been in jail.

"Oh yeah, he's been in jail for punching his boss." said Ellen, "see, for that he gets arrested and jail time, not punching his wife around."

"I see," sighed Laura.

"Besides punching a boss, he as punched a parole

officer, and Mark said he would like to punch that pest of a detective who has kept track of his life ever since he got out of jail after serving his time. He always said he wanted to get that detective, that it was personal now. He wasn't like that at all years ago when I first met him, or if he was, he certainly hid it well."

"So where did you meet him?" asked Laura curiously wanting to know their history to get a background on the ways of her husband.

"In a bar, of course. And of course, he was about two sheets to the wind drunk and flirtatious as hell. But, I was drinking too, so there you have it. Anyway, we started to date, casual at first, but then it wasn't long thereafter I got pregnant, so we got married. He was good with our son. Mark worked at the refinery back then and made good money, and stayed sober. I was working as a hairdresser full time when we met and got married, then I worked part time after our son was born. We were busy working, both of us, and with a child and all, everything was routine. We got along pretty well. And he kept out of trouble. But when our son was grown up and out on his own, it seemed Mark drank more. Everything got worse. He was nasty to me when he woke up with a hangover, being mad, wanting to start fights. It is why I like riding my bike. I could just leave him sit and jump on my bike and go for a ride. It's the best way to calm my nerves, clear my head, and get a good work out all at the same time," declared Ellen sounding depressed. "If only I could divorce his sorry ass. But I am afraid if I try, he will find a way to kill me."

"How about arsenic, or anti-freeze in his beer," suggested Laura. "Oh, but wait a minute, those methods take too long and leave toxic telltale traces in body tissue; that is, if for some reason, some court should order an autopsy after the deed is done."

The two women sat for a while longer making pretend revenge plans regarding Mark. Another Danish and cup of coffee added more sugar and caffeinated fuel to their already creative eagerness. Laura was just a bystander, more or less trying to help her friend feel better by making up creative plots. They were just getting their kicks, pretending to get revenge. But little did Laura know that Ellen was listening carefully and actually became more serious thinking about the possibility of actually getting away with murder. Her thoughts were of getting her revenge on her horrible abusive husband. They sat each in deep thought when Ellen suddenly noticed what time it was getting to be.

"It's time to go," Ellen suddenly sounded frantic, "he'll be home soon. I'm late already for getting dinner on the table by the time he gets home." She jumped up, said a quick good-bye and raced out the cafe door, nearly tripping on the steps. Laura stood at the entrance to the cafe and watched Ellen quickly yank her bike from the bike rack, hop on it and head out onto the street. She gave a quick wave good-bye and hurriedly rode off heading in the direction of her house.

Chapter Six

Ellen rode her bike hard and fast to get home. She quickly got things out of the refrigerator and started dinner. She hurried and got things on the table in time. But this evening Mark was later than usual.

"Where is my dinner?" Mark was angry when he got home, staggered in the kitchen door, bouncing off the walls he was so drunk. Ellen was supposed to have his dinner on the table when he got home. And he was usually home after he stopped off to have a few beers with his work buddies when they got off work, but this time he was really late, so Laura had cleared the table and put all the food in the refrigerator so it wouldn't spoil.

"It's in the refrigerator. I can warm it up for you."

"I told you I would be home by six."

"It's seven." She protested in a low voice standing at the refrigerator with her back to him. He heard her and just glared at her. When he stood next to her, she felt nauseous. He smelled of beer and cheat perfume. She knew he was messing around. She saw the red lipstick on his light blue work shirt collar. It disgusted her. She wanted out.

"Shut your smart mouth, or I'll shut it for you." He couldn't resist and at that moment, he wanted to strangle her. It was all he could do to hold it together to keep from letting her have it. He felt dizzy for a second. He drank too much on an empty stomach. He had skipped lunch, as his girlfriend had come to his truck at his work site for a quickie visit.

Ellen ignored the last comment and began putting the left-over dinner containers in the microwave to heat up the food for him.

"Get me a beer," Mark ordered Ellen. And in that second something happened in Ellen's mind. She had just reached her limit of patience with this man, and she decided she was going to do something about it. But what, how, and when, she had no idea.

Chapter Seven

The next day when Ellen met Laura at the coffee shop on De Mun Blvd. With coffee and pastries in hand they sat huddled together, sharing their ideas and proceeded to plan Mark's demise.

"Why are you helping me with this?" asked Ellen.

"I like you," answered Laura, "and working with my detective husband behind the scenes all those years, I got the taste for it, for the psychological mystery of crime and why it's committed. And for the fact that just too many women were abused in marriages, and I guess I got tired of seeing it. I enjoyed helping my husband, Hank, on cases it was a very special time for us. I treasure those memories of us working together to solve a case. I got to use my intuition and psychic skills. Hank always said I should have been on the payroll. He said it just worked out for him to run the cases he was working on past me. He said I always seemed to offer good insightful suggestions, and ideas. We operated as a team. And in the end, when he passed, his fellow officers who attended the funeral told me he was the best detective on the force, ever. I don't think they were just being kind. My husband solved a lot of cases and in record time, some with my help, of course, I am proud to say. There are a lot of bad people in jail because of his good work--I mean 'our' good work."

Ellen felt fortunate to meet Laura, she needed all the emotional support and help she could gather because Mark was getting on Ellen's last nerve.

"I almost pushed him down the basement steps this morning, I was so mad," sighed Ellen, "I just wish I could leave him. But I do believe if I do, he will find me and kill me."

"Where does your son live?" asked Laura, wondering if he could offer her any refuge or help.

"My son and his wife live in Portland, Oregon," sighed Ellen, "guess I could visit him. I really do not want to impose on their busy lives, though. Besides, it doesn't solve anything. Mark will still be in the picture, I would only be putting off the unavoidable inevitable. And, it would just be my luck, Mark would say he wanted to come along with me on the trip to see his son, then what?"

"Well, that won't work then," said Laura. "I found several of the cases my husband worked on were about abused wives who tried to leave or hit back in retaliation, only to be found buried in the back yard or wrapped in plastic in the freezer in the basement. So, I don't advise that either. Also, in many cases we worked on, the wives were murdered because the husband had a new girlfriend. You know out with the old, in with the new," Laura joked but it wasn't funny to either of them.

"Well, I couldn't help but notice lately, besides seeing the lipstick on his collar, that there was the scent of cheap perfume infused with the stale smell of beer. And last evening he came home much later than usual. He said he was having beers with the boys after work, but I saw a fresh shade of pink lipstick was on his cheek and collar."

"I guess we could follow him one day, just for grins," suggested Laura. She loved detective work she was eager to get back into action in the field.

"I have no car. He won't let me work, so he says I don't need a car, what do I need a car for?" Ellen was practically beside herself with despair and hopelessness.

"I have a car," offered Laura smiling with a mischievous look in her big green eyes.

"Well, then shall we?" suggested Ellen smiling. Laura shared her idea then.

"In the morning, I'll be around the corner from your house, keeping an eye on his truck to watch what time he leaves for work," suggested Laura. "As soon as he heads to his truck, you come running out the back way from your house and jump into my car and we'll follow him." A plan was in place. The ladies were excited with their upcoming adventure, and Ellen's spirits were lifted.

"Sounds good to me," said Ellen, "I really appreciate you for being my friend and for helping me."

"Hey, it's just a walk in the park, right?" smiled

Laura. She picked that saying up from Hank, then was reminded of it when Ellen used it one day as she and Laura were walking Emma in Forest Park and a car driven by a reckless youth nearly sideswiped them. They laughed at Ellen's comment and somehow it just stuck with them to be used whenever a silly near narrow escape sprung them into action.

Chapter Eight

The next morning, bright and early, Laura with Emma, in the back seat, fully alert, sat watching the big red truck. They sat in Laura's Prius near Ellen's house. Laura kept her eyes peeled on the house and the truck parked in the driveway. Laura sat nervously staring at the house and truck watching for any signs of movement. As she stared at the obnoxious big red dual-wheeled truck, she could not help but wonder what horrific deficiency in the size of a male's member, would provoke someone to buy such a super-sized gas guzzling, biggest pick-up truck ever made. The longer she stared at the dual rear wheels, she wondered what the purpose of all that was. And why the added bodacious audacity of the horrible reflective, extra-large, naked lady mud flaps? They had to be blinding to a driver following close behind at night, with headlights reflected back to the driver. It amazed her. Her day-dreamy thoughts were suddenly interrupted as she saw movement at the house.

Laura saw Mark come out of their house and get in his truck. Then one second later, Ellen came running like a marathoner out the back door of the house, racing through the yard, spotting Laura's Prius she ran to it and jumped into the passenger seat. They watched the truck pull out and slowly followed it. Laura kept a safe distance of several car lengths behind when they got onto busier streets. They followed Mark for several miles meandering through residential neighborhoods. Laura followed at a distance then pulled over and parked as she saw Mark pull over and park at his job at a new condominium complex construction site near the corner of Clayton and Hanley roads. Mark and the other workers were helping build forms for pouring concrete. About a half block away, Laura, Ellen and Emma sat in Laura's Prius just out of sight and prepared to sit and watch him work.

"We should have brought snacks," declared Ellen as if they were attending a drive-in movie. In a way it did feel like they were watching a construction training video as they with collective interest watched the workers go about the process of building. The ladies had to marvel at the guys who worked up high on the multi floored tall structure.

"That job would definitely not be for me," declared Ellen, "I am afraid of heights along with my fear of close spaces."

"I know what you mean," agreed Laura, she had always marveled at high-rise construction workers' nerve and true grit. As if they were watching a movie, the need for food or snacks popped into her minds again.

"Oh, I almost forgot, there is a cooler on the floor behind me with sandwiches, potato chips, fruit and snacks. I also brought a big thermos of coffee and I have a couple of cheese Danish pastries we can have now and then lunch for later," stated Laura.

"Oh cool, thanks," smiled Ellen. "You think of everything," she added as she reached behind Laura's seat to open the lid of the cooler where all the goodies were stored and smiled at the wide variety of treats. It was still breakfast time, so she grabbed the thermos and the pastries and a few treats and some water for Emma. They ate pastry and sipped coffee while they watched Mark work.

"Just a walk in the park," smiled Ellen. "I have decided I love watching people work, building and creating, especially when I can just sip coffee, eat pastry and just watch." They both had to laugh.

"Can't beat it," Laura agreed.

"Mark actually looks like he is working and contributing," observed Ellen.

"Changing your mind about him, are you?" Laura questioned rather teasingly.

"I wouldn't go that far," replied Ellen, then she had to smile. She was willing to give credit where credit was due amongst all the negativity she saw and experienced.

They sat for what seemed like a long time. It was getting close to lunch time and they were thinking about pulling away and taking Emma for a walk back at the park, when they noticed an old beat-up car pulled up and parked a little way away. They observed a skinny blonde in a tank top and short skirt get out of the beat-up car. She walked with a wiggle as she strolled up to Mark's truck. She readily opened the unlocked driver's side door and climbed in. She did not drive off in the truck, so it appeared that she was planning to just sit and wait in the truck. The ladies were amazed at the sudden twist in the dull construction video they thought they were boringly observing. Laura and Ellen both whipped out their smart phones and shot videos and took pictures of the little blonde as she got out of her car and walked toward Mark's truck. Even Emma's ears perked up and she sat looking straight ahead through the windshield. She sat fully alert and made little whimpering sounds.

The ladies took lots of divorce evidence videos and photos. It wasn't long after, that it appeared to be lunchtime as they heard the sound of a whistle, and watched the workers disperse in all directions to their vehicles.

The ladies watched and snapped more photos and shot more video of Mark picking up his pace and smiling as he neared his truck and saw the pretty girl waiting for him to come inside. The ladies were appalled as they saw Mark kiss the rather young-looking girl who sat behind the steering wheel waiting for him. Mark had a big smile on his face as he slid into the truck and she scooted over a bit to let him in. It was difficult to tell but both ladies knew that the couple was stirring to get positioned for a quick afternoon delight.

"No wonder he wanted the biggest truck Ford ever

made, more room to maneuver around in, I guess." Ellen was clearly upset at the sight.

"Oh my, I'm glad we have photos and video," exclaimed Laura. She was silently not making any remarks about it, but she was clearly loving stake-out spying detective work.

"I feel like a fool. Why doesn't he just divorce me and get it over with so we can both move on," stated Ellen. "I can't figure that out."

"I guess it's just fun sneaking around, and it gives him a sense of power over you, cheating on you, rubbing salt into your wounds, and using you has a punching bag. I guess he doesn't want to give that up." Laura felt bad and was feeling Ellen's pain.

"What an asshole he turned out to be," were the only words that Ellen could conjure up at the moment.

Laura could readily sympathize as she only knew too well how it felt to be cheated on. Before she met and married her wonderful husband Hank, she was engaged to a man who cheated on her, even while they were planning their wedding. As soon as her best friend found out about her finance cheating on her, she told Laura and Laura was glad she told her, although the news hurt like hell. It was a difficult time, but she was so glad she found out before she married him. She immediately broke off the engagement and cancelled the wedding. So Laura knew from experience too, how it felt to be cheated on. So a little vicarious revenge would do her spirit good too.

Chapter Nine

They sat and watched the commotion in the big red pickup truck for about thirty minutes till they couldn't stand it anymore. They turned the car around and headed back to Laura's place and took Emma for a walk. They decided they needed more java, so after Emma's walk, they left Emma at home and headed to the coffee shop on De Mun Blvd. They wanted to talk more about possible ideas and plans. When they arrived, they waited a bit in line and got their cups of coffee. They decided outdoors was best, and sat at a table on the patio, it being such a lovely day, and the patio was less crowded and more private than sitting inside.

"If we divorce, the house goes up for sale, and I should get half of everything. But, if he has an accident and dies, I get everything," Ellen noted with tears in her eyes. She felt worse than an idiot. "So he's punching on me and cheating on me. What the hell am I doing with this maniac in my life? Amazon is hiring at their new distribution center in Fenton and I have just applied for a job there. It's time to move on from this messy stage of my life," declared Ellen, she was determined to change her life for the better.

"Just a walk in the park," smiled Laura, "isn't that what you always say?"

"Yes, it is, and making a break of the old and beginning a new plan will be just that." Ellen was beginning to feel better already.

"Why don't you just leave him, now?" encouraged Laura.

"What?"

"You can stay with me, my condo is a two-bedroom, two-bath. Leave him, stay with me, and file for divorce. Papers can be served to him, and you don't want to be there when he gets served, anyway. He'll kill you. So come stay with me. A divorce lawyer is easy enough to find. What do you think? Let's go to your house, while Mark is at work, and grab a few of your clothes and things; your bike, bike clothes and gear. But let's not make it look like you left him. Just take a few things so it looks like you went for a bike ride and disappeared into thin air. Don't answer your phone if he calls you.

"That does sound like a good plan, thank you so much for offering," Ellen was very grateful. "Are you sure?"

"Yes, I am sure," answered Laura, "you need to be in a safe place, and I would love the company as it has been just too quiet since Hank is not with me any longer."

Ellen quickly made a mental list of the few things that she wanted to get from her house. She was not planning on taking much, just a few clothes for a new job that she hoped to get, and her electronics was all that she needed, just her day-to-day stuff. For sure she wanted to take her biking clothes, helmet, riding gloves, riding shoes, and her bike. Laura folded down her back seats and Ellen's road bike easily slid in and fit in Laura's Prius hatch back, even without taking the front wheel off. They quickly packed the things Ellen wanted to take into trash bags and were out of the house in minutes.

"Whatever else I need I will worry about later," Ellen just wanted to leave and get away from the horrible negative energy she felt permeated the house.

"I know he doesn't let you have much cash," stated Laura, "I can help you out."

"He gives me a measly small allowance, just enough really for buying groceries," shared Ellen. "But I have been buying him more of the on-sale cheap, not good for you at all, GMO grain raised, shot up on antibiotics, feed-lot meats, and other cheap foods made with lots of toxic high fructose corn syrup and lots of preservatives. I buy him the cheap stuff so I can hold back and keep some of the grocery money for myself and hide it," revealed Ellen. "That cheap food is toxic, so it suits him well. Funny if I tried to poison someone I'd be put in jail, but these big corporations run the government and have the now-useless FDA bought and stored in their back pockets. So, they get a free pass to poison all of us especially poor people who cannot afford better food.

What kind of a Reptilian brained, monstrous patriarchal rule world do we live in? All I see is that the corrupt medical system wants to wreck immune systems, causing illness, then keep the patients hanging on with pills and surgeries until their bank accounts are drained from ever increasing medical expenses. Cures, there are no cures, it's plain to me that the whole Reptilian brain of the New World Order secret societies want to depopulate, to thin the herd. I have read where over a hundred-thousand people die each year from taking medications as prescribed, you'll never hear that on the evening news will you?" said Ellen and Laura could not help but agree. Ellen felt better after her rant. Not being allowed to work, she read a lot and watched fascinating interviews on *Open Minds* GAIA TV.

"We are on the same page, my friend," smiled Laura as she packed Ellen's belongings in the car. "When it comes to our ideas about evil Illuminati Reptilian Hybrids wanting to band natural supplements and insist on pushing questionable vaccine injections that bypass and threaten the abilities of our natural immune system's safe-guards. They use the bought and owned media, no longer just by brainwashing commercials, but now in the evening news itself, to push through their for big-profit toxic agendas. While the informed portion of the population is on to the Reptilian Hybrids agenda to take their planet back. And yes, they are aware that a human depopulation agenda exists.

"Oh yes, I watch GAIA television Interviews too," admitted Laura proudly, "my detective mind says it pays to know who your enemies are and to learn the motives of both sides of the story."

"I'm so glad that we are like minded," smiled Ellen.

"Life is just a walk in the park, right?" Laura replied. She and Ellen had lots of things in common, including using that particular phrase to lift their spirits from time to time.

"Did you gather everything on your list and get it into the car?" asked Laura.

"Yes, I believe I did. Just a walk in the park, fitting everything into your Prius. No problems at all." She was excited to begin a new life with a new job, a new friend, and finally become an independent free woman. It was time.

Chapter Ten

"Okay, I have contacted my son's divorce attorney, Doris Dewey," confirmed Laura the next morning as they sat on the patio having coffee.

"What did she have to say," asked Ellen eager to get the divorce process going.

"She said that she can come by later this morning and talk to you and get those divorce papers drawn up. The sooner he is served the better, she said. I emailed her copies of the videos and pictures we took."

"This is good. Things are moving right along," Ellen smiled, and she was grateful. Ellen was acclimating and becoming more comfortable staying at Laura's as the days went on. And with the added news that the lawyer was coming over soon, she was beginning to feel even better. "This is so nice. Your condo is just lovely. I have always wondered what these condos were like. What a great location too, right across the street from the park."

"I'm glad I have the extra room," sighed Laura, "Hank used to use that room for his office. And we would sit at his desk for hours sometimes, going through evidence and looking at clues while working on criminal cases. I miss him and the work."

"I can tell you have a bit of a detective in you," Ellen said as they enjoyed their coffee and pastry on the patio. It was such a lovely morning.

Later that morning, Ellen made a freshly brewed pot of coffee. She put cookies on the table and got busy getting things set up for the lawyer's visit.

Doris Dewey was a silver-haired, sharp-tongued, middle-aged, woman of stocky stature with a deep voice and a determined personality. Any woman who had Doris Dewey for her divorce attorney usually came out on the winning end of a divorce. She usually got the most possessions and most awarded alimony for her clients. Doris Dewey, Attorney at Law, sometimes had potential clients waiting in line for her services. So, the ladies felt lucky to be able to meet with her so soon. The ladies were immediately impressed by her straight talk, forward thinking, and strategical planning techniques. She looked at the photos and videos of Mark and his girlfriend. She listened to Ellen's stories about her abusive husband harassing, slapping and punching her. She saw Ellen's pictures of bruises and cuts and black eyes. Ellen even had voice recordings of Mark screaming hateful remarks and threatening her.

"Oh, you did good getting these recordings, photos of your injuries, and videos and of the girlfriend," declared Doris Dewey, "You should get everything and alimony, no problem. You have sufficient evidence of physical and mental cruelty."

"That's good to hear," replied Ellen.

"Have you ever had to have him arrested for spousal abuse? If so we can get the record and that would also be a sure win for our your case."

"No, I have always been too afraid of having the police arrest him," Ellen said through tear filled eyes."

"I understand," replied Doris with a sympathetic tone.

"How soon can you serve the papers?" wondered Ellen.

"As early as tomorrow or the day after," Doris Dewey said, "we work fast in cases such as this. We want you to be safe."

"Will I have to face him in court?" wondered Ellen, she was becoming more afraid of Mark every day. She didn't want to be in the same room with him, much less sleep with him, which was why she was always glad they had the largest king-size bed ever made. Most of the time during the night she would get up and lay on the couch then get back in bed before he woke up. His snoring was becoming worse, and he had sleep apnea which was even worse to listen to. Of course, he was in denial and would not make any effort to go to the doctor. Didn't matter, as of late she really did not even want him to see a doctor, thinking maybe his labored breathing would one day do him in.

Over time, Ellen mostly just stayed quiet as a mouse around him, as she did not trust when his sudden and unpredictable erratic outbursts of anger would occur. It was what was so unnerving, one day or one minute, he could almost actually be nice, and the next day or the next minute, she could be shocked into traumatic reality and excruciating pain by a lightning fast backhanded slap across the face. He would strike her when the urge presented itself. It could happen at any time for any reason like maybe he thought the bacon was not done enough, or too crispy or burnt. She could never get it right, because no matter how she prepared the bacon, it was never right and never suited him. Her stress levels were so high they were about to impact her health in every way. Her hair was already thinning, her skin was bad. Her stomach ached all the time. Anymore, any fearful thought of him made her nauseous. It was indeed time to get out of the marriage.

Chapter Eleven

"I feel so much better," smiled Ellen after the attorney left the condo. "I feel like a weight has been lifted off my shoulders. Also, I heard from my son a few minutes ago and he is so glad that I am taking the necessary steps to free myself from Mark. Mark never really took the time to get to know our son as a young man, and I guess that is just as well. My son and his wife just moved to Portland, Oregon and love it there. I am so happy for them and their new beginning, seems we are both experiencing periods of change and modifications, and this is good."

"I'm so glad things are looking up for you and your son," agreed Laura. "I heard from my son, Bob, yesterday, he misses his father terribly, as do I. My son appears to be a true product of two self-proclaimed detectives, so it's no wonder he is a detective with the St. Louis Police Department as his father was. I want grandchildren, but I don't know if having children is part of his and his finance's plans. This will be a second marriage for both of them. I would love grandchildren, but I realize people have to do what they see is right for them to do. I just want him to be happy and safe."

It was such a beautiful day that the ladies took Emma for a walk around the neighborhood.

"Let's walk up to Panera's and sit outside," suggested Ellen.

"That's a lovely idea," replied Laura, "we can take Emma, if we sit at an outside table."

Emma was Laura's beloved Rottweiler. The humane society where she got her said that Emma came from a loving family, but could no longer keep her as they already had a German Shepard and the two dogs did not get along. Emma was about five or six years old when Laura got her, and she was very well trained. Laura was always afraid she would mess up her training, but Emma never forgot her lessons. Emma would never enter a doorway unless Laura said it was okay. She would never race pass Laura either going up or down the steps. And if she did something wrong, like scratch on the patio screen when she wanted back inside, Laura just had to show her by holding her paw and saying no scratching here on the screen, but it's okay to scratch over here on the wood. She only had to show and tell her that one time. Emma never forgot her lesson. She was smart and Laura always felt very protective whenever Emma was by her side.

Emma had only one bad habit, she did not like the big, tall mailman who walked close by the front window everyday as he cut across the lawn to the next condo's front door. Laura wasn't sure if it was because he came so close to the window when he cut across the front yard, or because he wore a uniform. Either way, Laura made sure to block Emma from the front window by placing a table and lamp there, so Emma would stay back from the window and not scratch at it when the mailman showed up. That seemed to be the one bad habit that Laura could not end with Emma. But that was okay as the table lamp barricade seemed to work, she still barked, but at least she could not get to the window.

Laura wished the mailman would walk out a bit from the front window, then Laura thought Emma would not carry on as much. Evidently, the postman was not afraid of the barking and carrying on by Emma. Laura could never understand this, why incite the dog, she wondered. The way it was, Laura almost felt like the mailman was daring and tempting Emma to charge through the glass window at him. In any case, Emma was a good watch dog, and maybe that was a good thing with the likes of Mark looming in her and Ellen's atmosphere. Ellen hoped it would not be much longer, and the divorce papers would be served and hopefully soon the divorce would be final.

Chapter Twelve

"Doris just called," said Ellen with an anxious tone in her voice, "Mark has been served. I wonder how he is going to take it?" Ellen sounded concerned.

"Well, he doesn't know where you are living, so we can still feel that you are safe being here with me," replied Laura. Yet they were still being safety minded.

So just in case, the ladies were very mindful of their every move. It seemed as if they were always looking over their shoulders to see if that big red pickup truck was lurking anywhere nearby. Little did they know that Mark was beginning to have more problems of his own besides being served divorce papers.

Chapter Thirteen

"Well, I'll be damned," grinned Mark, "I was wondering where she went off to. That bitch done got herself a divorce filed against me." In a way Mark was sorry, yeah sorry to lose his punching bag. Whenever work was horrible it was so nice to come home after a few beers with the boys and have a little fun kicking around and picking on Ellen. It was fun to get her all riled up. Mark loved seeing the look of fear in her eyes when he yelled and came after her for doing just any little thing he did not like. It could be from the way she made coffee to burning the bacon, as he always described it. Seemed to him she could never please him with anything.

Mark had another problem now to deal with, seems his young little girlfriend, Sally, told him at lunch when she met him in his truck at work, that she done got herself knocked up. This bit of news on top of the divorce papers made Mark feel extra on edge, mad and nervous. Now that his wife wanted to divorce him, he knew that he was going to feel pressured by Sally into marrying her. He didn't want a kid to raise. Why did she have to go and spoil all the wonderful afternoon fun they had when she came to his work site.

Mark had to put a plan in place. He was distracted now; his biggest problem was the girlfriend. He was too distracted to protest or do anything about Ellen wanting a divorce. He did not plan on contesting the divorce in court because he did not plan on signing the divorce papers or ever appearing in court. He would deal with Ellen in his own fashion after he dealt with the girlfriend. No way did he want to be married and support a pregnant wife and then raise and support a kid for the next twenty years, or longer, if the kid turns out to be a lazy bum.

Mark was in the kitchen getting another beer, after having a few drinks with the boys after work, when he heard a loud knock at the back door. He looked out the window and saw the little blonde at the door. Sally drove an old used multi-colored door, dented fender, fit for the junkyard, Chevy. He saw it parked in the driveway. He felt a sudden toxic emotional cocktail of sexual desire and hate, all mixed together in a dangerous concoction, fueled by already too many beers which were making him feel slightly lightheaded and off balance.

"What are you doing here, darling?" he sarcastically asked when he opened the door to let her in. He tried desperately to dampen down the sexual desire he felt when she strolled past him in her tank top and short cut-off jeans. Her eyes bright with sparkling makeup and her long blonde hair hanging down her back in big curls.

"I thought I would just follow you home from the bar," Sally answered.

"So why did you come by the bar?" he asked.

"I saw your truck there as I drove by, stalking you," she added with a teasing smile." So I got thirsty and came in for a beer. I didn't bother you while you were with your buddies, did I? I knew you all were talking about your work. I could hear you from across the room."

"I saw you sitting way over there at the corner of the bar," Mark said taking her by the arm and leading her to the kitchen.

"Want a beer?" he offered.

"I would love a beer," she accepted with a smile. At the bar she had kept her distance, as she did not want to infringe on Mark's time with his buddies. She merely observed them from a distance and watched them, intrigued by their male-bonding joking and wise-cracking interactions, as they all stood at the bar talking about what went wrong with the broken concert mixer that hosed up their scheduled lists of accomplishments for that day.

"Come let's sit in the living room," suggested Mark as he handed her the beer.

"I want to talk about us," revealed Sally, as she raised the bottle to her mouth to take a long sip of cold refreshing brew. The fizz and saltiness tickled her parched dry throat as it went down. She was a little nervous. And then she remembered that she really should not be drinking alcohol if she were indeed pregnant, oops.

"Oh, you do?" Mark was more drunk than usual, and he was beginning to slur his words.

"Have you forgotten that I am pregnant?" she reminded him as soon as they sat down together on the couch.

Mark felt like he had been punched in the gut. He was certainly too old for all of this crap. No way was he going to raise a kid at this time in his life. He wondered why she would even think that he would be interested. His life had enough challenges in it for now with Ellen wanting to divorce him. It wasn't that she left him; rather, it was the idea of having to sell the house and give half of everything to her. If she died, there would be no reason for a divorce. Same with his crazy girlfriend Sally thinking she could trap a well-paid construction worker into marriage. No way!

"What did you say?" Mark wanted to draw the moment out, giving himself time to think of excuses and answers both.

"Remember, I'm pregnant, Mark," she repeated in a perky voice, as if she thought that he should be thrilled. But it looked like he was not thrilled, not at all, more like he had the dreadful look of a burden to deal with, or a trap ready to lock him in a prison of duty, and unwanted responsibility.

"Look, baby, I'm too old, to be starting with all of this," and he meant it.

"You love me, don't you?" Sally asked, she was setting the trap and she knew it. Actually, she wasn't pregnant, she just wanted to trap him, keep him all to herself. She had a plan where they would get married right away, and then soon after they were married, she would just report an unfortunate miscarriage.

"I really do not think that I want to be a father or even want to get married," Mark was open and blunt, and he knew she did not like what she was hearing. Sally was homeless before she came to St. Louis and got the job at McDonald's and moved into and shared a co-worker's apartment. Her parents had thrown her out for" using drugs and hanging out with hoodlums," those were their words. Sally denied their allegations profusely. But her parents would not listen and threw her out onto the streets. She went to her boyfriend, she thought she could stay with him, but he had found someone else shortly after she moved in and threw her out into the streets too. So Sally jumped on a bus. She had just enough money for a ticket that took her as far as St. Louis. She was quick to get work at McDonald's, but she hated it. She wanted to be a stay-at-home wife and mother and feel the security of a working husband who made good money. She figured she had to depend on a man for her livelihood, because it seemed she could not find a good paying job for herself. She thought that she might find a stable future with Mark, but she soon realized that she was only dreaming.

"But," Sally began to cry. Shedding a few tears was her last attempt at persuasion and she could immediately see it was not going to work with Mark. Next, she would try anger and demand what she wanted.

"I think you should get an abortion," Mark said with stern affirmation. He wanted her to realize that he truly meant it. He was not going to raise a kid.

"But it's your baby," pleaded Sally, she could not understand why he would not want to raise his own kid. But apparently, he had doubts about being the real father.

"Oh, really, for sure," snapped Mark, "I am the father, really, for sure?" He wanted to get the point across. How could he be sure she wasn't screwing the whole neighborhood.

"Yes, for sure," she swore through fake tears, "you are the father." Anyone observing these two characters would come to the conclusion that they were actually well matched as one was as untruthful and ruthless as the other.

"You're just a whore," he accused her, and he said it because he knew that it would get her going. He wanted to ruffle her feathers to get her mad so she would storm out the door and he would never see her again. At this very moment he hated all women, and silently vowed never to mess with or be taken in by another floozie like her again.

"You bastard!" She wasn't going to just sit there and take this. She swung at him and missed. He laughed in her face. So then she threw her empty beer bottle at him. Big mistake, she immediately realized, as nearly getting hit in the face with a beer bottle made him very very mad, and she knew he was drunk, which made it much worse. His temper flared. This frightened her. And it was too late for her to get out of there, and she knew it.

"You f'ing bitch," he swore at her then backhanded her a good one across the face. The blow sent her flying off the couch onto the floor. Her face hurt like hell where he hit her. She just wanted to get out of this crazy man's house. On her hands and knees she attempted to crawl pass him toward the door. He could hear her sniffling and crying as she crawled away. Crawling like a dog she was, he thought, and this infuriated him. So he came up behind her and kicked her rear end, and she fell over and curled up in pain. He went after her, and with his steel toed work boot kicked her a good one in the stomach.

"There, that one is for the baby," he groaned and sounded like some kind of sick demented animal. He was outraged. This little bitch was not going to mess up his life. These bitches are a dime a dozen, I'll find more where this one came from.

"Oh, you're killing me," she moaned. The look in his eyes, froze her heart with fear. For then he reached down, and with both hands grabbed her around the neck, enough to raise her head up high enough. Then with his right hand he delivered a blow with such force to her jaw that she flew against the pointed corner of the coffee table. She slumped back down to the floor, dead.

Chapter Fourteen

"Now what, come on get up you bitch," he demanded, "get up I say." Even though he saw the blood running down her face and covering her white tank top. In his most drunken anger outrage, he just knew she was faking it.

"Get up," he demanded! "Get up," he screamed but only he could hear his demanding words.

"Crap," now he would have to do something with this damn body. "Think, I have to think." He demanded his fuzzy booze-soaked brain to think.

"Think," he commanded out loud to his brain.

In a panic, he pushed aside the coffee table, and yanked the area rug out from under the two recliners front legs that rested on it. He rolled her body up in the rug, tight. She was small, so even staggering drunk it would be easy for him to carry her outside and throw her in the bed of his pickup truck, and he did just that. But he forgot one thing, her old wreck of a car blocked his truck from leaving the driveway.

"Damn," he moaned to himself. He would have to do something about that car. Then he thought that he might as well keep both of them together. So he retrieved the rolled-up area rug with her in it back out from the bed of the truck. Dropped it on the ground and unrolled it, then searched through her pockets. He needed to find the keys to her car, as he did not find them in the ignition, under the seat, or under the floor mat. His foggy brain was hard at work, plus he had a horrible headache coming on. The plan was to find her keys, put her body in her car trunk, and dump both car and her body in some isolated area. He searched her pants pockets. Finally, he found her keys in one of the pockets along with her cash in in the other front pocket of her pants. He found her cell phone and wallet in her back pockets. He left her phone and wallet with her. He rolled her back up in the rug and put it in the trunk of her car, slammed the trunk lid, jumped in the driver's seat.

He was nervous hoping the car would start. As it was, it took several tries, but he finally got the car started, and backed out of the driveway. He wasn't quite sure where he was going to abandon the car. Up north he thought, maybe somewhere near the airport where he could take the MetroLink back to the Clayton stop near his house.

He nervously drove the old wreck of a car. It ran badly, he hoped it would get him to where he wanted to go. He drove around a bit then picked a rather bad area near the airport, he turned onto what he thought was a service road. He saw the MetroLink station about a mile up ahead, across a mostly weeded and grassy field. He could easily walk that distance he thought. He decided he wanted to make it look like an auto accident had happened. He was drunk, nervous, and not thinking very clearly. In a sudden frantic motion, he stopped in the middle of the road where he saw the ditch looked the deepest. He backed up bit, and when he had the car perpendicular to the ditch, he gunned the engine and squealed the tires and drove nose first into the ditch. It was steeper than what he thought, and the car landed with a hard bang crumbling the front end. He hit his head on the visor and corner of the mirror. It hurt like hell, as did his chest and ribs from slamming against the steering wheel.

Big mistake he thought, he should have put her behind the wheel, put the car in drive and just sent her in the ditch. But it was too late for a do-over. Rubbing his aching head, he cursed himself for making a bad decision to crash the car with him in it. What was he thinking? Now he had to get himself out of the car and climb up and out of the ditch to get her out of the trunk and put her behind the steering wheel.

"Damn," was all he could muster. His driver side door was buckled a bit at the hinges. It took all his might to open it just a bit. Then turning a bit sideways he used both feet to try to force the door open wide enough for him to fit through. He leaned against it then with his shoulder. He banged his shoulder against it a couple of times till it suddenly flopped all the way open. He had a heck of a time getting out of the car without his feet slipping and sliding deeper into the ditch and in the mud. He struggled and somehow crawled out and up on his hands and knees, slipping and sliding. He had to kick and dig the toes of his work shoes in the soft soil to work his way out and up to the back of the car. Somehow, he managed to crawl out and out of the ditch. He had to stop and rest a minute. Finally, he crawled up enough to get behind the car and to open the trunk. He was so glad he thought to take the keys out of the ignition with him when he climbed out of the car in order to open the trunk. He lifted the carpet roll out of the trunk easily enough. He proceeded to unroll her body from the area rug and drag her body down in the ditch, slipping and sliding with her, and put her in the car and prop her up against the steering wheel. He then remembered to put the keys back in the ignition and turn it to the on position. He crawled back up out of the ditch while trying to smooth out his footprints along the way.

Working his way behind the car he carefully rolled up the rug. He looked around for the best spot to dispose of the rug. He thought that he saw a good enough place, so he carried the rolled up rug over to a nearby wooded area and shoved it in and under tall weeds, brush, and leaves surrounding a thick growth of trees. Amazingly he did not get blood from the rug on himself. Well he got a little blood on his jeans, but they were dark denim and it didn't show up too bad. He was just glad he didn't get blood on his shirt. He did not want people staring at him on the MetroLink train ride back to the Clayton stop. He could easily then walk the rest of the way home to his house.

He walked through the open field toward the MetroLink station about a mile away. It did not take him long to walk through the tall grass and weeds. When he got to the platform, he reached in his pockets for the dollar bills he took from Sally's pockets and quickly bought his ticket. He only had to wait a minute or two for a southbound train to arrive and approach the platform. Sitting on the train, he breathed a sigh of relief and closed his eyes for a moment to think and mentally retrace his steps in his head about what he had just done. Did he think of everything? And he felt as if he did. In the end he thought the whole ordeal went just fine. He was pleased. One down one to go, he thought. Ellen was next.

Chapter Fifteen

Laura and Ellen were enjoying a beautiful morning having breakfast on the patio. Laura loved having Ellen's company. Ellen was feeling better in general, she liked living with Laura. She felt safe there. She loved Emma. She loved the walks she and Laura would take with Emma in the park every day. But she was especially happy about getting hired on at the Amazon Distribution Center in Fenton. Laura loaned her the money for a down payment for a used Prius, so she could drive the twelve miles to and from work every day.

Ellen was beginning to feel like a real person once again. She had purpose and she loved her independence. It had been less than two weeks, and she had not heard a word from Mark, for which she was most grateful. She was grateful but she worried none the less, wondering what he was up to. Why were there no angry phone messages or texts. In a way, she was very surprised, but she did not want to think about it.

She did not want to put negative thoughts out there in the ether, because thoughts can become reality, and she did not want to even bring any psychic attention to any negative thoughts regarding Mark and what he was capable of doing, so she was grateful for the silence. Instead of worrying about the future and Mark, Ellen concentrated on living in the present moment enjoying her freedom and ability to get a job, and she enjoyed Emma and Laura's company, especially Laura's help and interest in her predicament with Mark.

When Laura wasn't out walking Emma, or riding her bike, she spent most of her days watching *Date Line*, reading mystery novels and catching up on the local news by reading the *St. Louis Post-Dispatch*. She liked to read the police report section, and there she came across an article about a young woman involved in a fatal accident on a service road near the airport. Her car ended up front first down in a deep ditch. The woman driver was pronounced deceased at the scene by the county coroner's office. Her name was Sally Adams according to the identification they found on her. According to the newspaper article, the authorities could not locate any next of kin. There was a picture in the paper of the car, showing the car nose down into a rather deep ditch, mainly the driver side and the rear of the car were visible in the photo. There was something about the picture of the car that looked very familiar to Laura, she thought she had just seen an old multi-colored door car like that somewhere recently.

"Ellen come look at this," directed Laura, holding up

the newspaper photo of the car in the ditch to the light in order to see it better.

Ellen was finished with her breakfast and was getting ready to go to her job at the Amazon Distribution Center. She was working the day shift because she was still in training. So far she thought she would really like the job, and the benefits were great, complete with health care, eye and dental coverage and her starting wages were over twenty-five dollars an hour. Ellen was thrilled to be on her own and out in the world. She was nervous at first, but easily adjusted. She loved learning and it was a joy to be around good hard-working people. She was all dressed and ready to leave when Laura asked to look at the picture.

"That car does look familiar," suggested Ellen, "is that the car the little blonde we saw drive up in at Mark's work location?"

"Yes, that's it!" Laura proclaimed with glee, "I think, you are correct." Laura got her cell phone out in order to bring up the pictures she took that day when she and Ellen went to spy on Mark at his work location.

"My gosh, look at this," said Laura, "it sure is the same car."

"That's very interesting," declared Ellen.

"Oh, here as I read on," said Laura, "it says, the coroner's office suspected foul play and detectives were investigating." Laura decided to call her son, Bob since he was a detective at the St. Louis Police department. She called him on speaker phone so Ellen could also hear what he had to say.

"Hi, Mom what can I do for you this morning?" asked her son, happy to help in any way he could.

"Hi dear, Ellen and I were just reading about the single car accident near the airport where it appears the young woman drove her car into the ditch.

"On that case," reported Bob, "I was just reading over that file."

"Well does anything seem a little off to you?" asked Laura?

"Yes, it does," replied Bob, "because according to the estimated time of death and the utility worker's statement who found her in the wrecked car, we do have reason to believe foul play was involved in her death. She may have died at an earlier time, at another location, and perhaps then her body and her car was taken to that location and made it look like an auto accident had taken place."

"That is very interesting," said Laura.

"Also, according to this report, investigating police officers searching the area found a rolled-up area rug, apparently recently discarded, complete with fairly fresh blood stains that with lab tests proved to be the same blood type as the woman's."

"Well, Ellen and I just compared the picture of the car in the newspaper to a picture I took when Ellen and I were staking-out Mark while he was at work. We sat in my car and watched him work and close to lunch time we were so surprised to see a young woman pulled up in her car and get out and wait in Mark's truck for him. The young woman was in the same car as what is in the newspaper. The cars look identical. They were easy to compare because both vehicles had the same mismatched painted driver side door, and the same old scrapes and dents on that side of the car, too.

"Well, that is very interesting indeed," suggested Bob, "forward those photos you have of her and her car meeting up with Mark, and I'll make a note and add them to her file."

"I'll keep digging and see what else I can come up with," added Laura before saying good-bye to her son and ending the call.

"The suspense is mounting isn't it. It's most interesting, indeed," remarked Ellen, checking the time then grabbing her jacket. "Well, I'm off to work, I'll see you later."

After Ellen left for work, Laura continued her research. Her mind was going a hundred miles an hour, she wanted to solve this case. What she wanted to see was the rug. She was sure the rug was locked up in evidence after the lab got through with it. Laura wanted to see the trunk of the car, too. She knew that the car would be in the police yard somewhere. Laura was going to have to call her son back and see if she could pay him a visit at his workplace. Actually, her crime solving mind was just eager to be a part of the investigation. She missed working with her detective husband, Hank, on his cases before he passed. He was a highly respected detective on the St. Louis police force just as their son, Bob, is now.

Chapter Sixteen

"Hi, Mom," said Bob to his mother on the phone. He was surprised to hear from her so soon again.

"I miss working with your father on cases, can I join you?" begged Laura her son Bob.

"Well, you know, Mom," Bob hesitated but only for a moment," I do work alone, so maybe I can accommodate your wishes." He smiled to himself, he knew his mother was a want-to-be detective and would be a great ride-along companion.

"Oh, son," replied Laura, "that would be wonderful." Oh, she was excited. What do I wear, she wondered. She got out her good pair of black walking shoes, put on her black slacks, and blue shirt.

"Why all I need is a few stripes and a badge, and I would fit right in," she said out loud to the full-length mirror in her bedroom, while tying her long hair back into a bum. Laura was all grins as she was going to love this day. And to be with her son was an extra bonus.

Laura thought her son was a chip off the old block of her loving and kind husband, Hank. He was tall and handsome like Hank was, too. She missed Hank but loved her son even more for being a good, decent man like Hank was.

Chapter Seventeen

Bob drove picked up his mother at her condo and then drove to the police evidence lot where Sally Adams' crashed car was being kept. The trunk, doors, and glove box were all open for inspection, ready to be examined. Bob and Laura pulled on rubber gloves and grabbed plenty of bags to fill with fiber samples. They brought their investigating kit filled with tweezers, magnifying glass, and a few other items. They were both eager and excited to be working together.

"Look, Bob, I see bits of some sort of fiber in the trunk" said Laura, as she used her tweezers and picked up pieces and held the sample up to her magnifying glass.

"It looks like carpet fiber, it's thick and course."

"It appears to be a red and gray tweed, doesn't it," suggested Laura.

"Sure would be interesting if it matched the fibers of the area rug found in the woods not far from the accident scene," said Bob. "And according to the forensic lab report we already know that the blood found on the rug matches Sally Adams' blood type.

They looked around the drivers and passenger's floor and seat area for more evidence. They found blond hair and dark hair fibers everywhere. They dusted for fingerprints and found both small, probably her prints, and they found larger prints that were man size. They were thrilled at the evidence they gathered. Things were beginning to come together.

Bob and Laura visited another evidence locker where the area rug was stored. They slowly slide it off the rack and carefully unrolled it on to the floor. They found matching rug fibers from the fibers on the rug and the fibers taken from the trunk of the wrecked car. Laura took pictures of the unrolled rug as well as the car and trunk.

"Bob, I am having a wonderful time," Laura said as she filled plastic bags with hair and fiber samples for the lab to check.

"Me too, Mom," Bob smiled as he rolled up the area rug and slide it back onto the shelf.

"It's such a lovely day," added Laura, and before she could continue Bob spoke as if he was reading her mind.

"It is, so how about we have lunch where we can sit outside and then drive out to the area near the airport where the incident happened," suggested Bob.

"That sounds like a wonderful idea," Laura was having the time of her life. They quickly packed things up and headed out to their car. They drove to the

Central West End, an affluent eclectic area just west of downtown near Forest Park

They sat outside at Dukes on Euclid Avenue and enjoyed bacon, lettuce and tomato sandwiches with thick golden home fries. It was such a lovely sunny day, perfect day for taking a little drive and walking the countryside.

"So Mom, what else have you been up too lately?" asked Bob taking a sip of his iced tea. He was enjoying the lunch and their time together.

"I have a roommate you know," informed Laura, "Ellen, she's very nice. I believe she has a son about your age. He and his wife just moved to Portland, Oregon."

"I had one of those once," smiled Bob, "a wife." He was sad over his recent divorce.

"I know son, I'm sorry about your divorce, but you are dating a lovely girl now, and I am sure that all will be fine," Laura took his hand for a moment, she saw the sadness in his eyes.

Bob perked up thinking about his lovely girlfriend. He knew that if he played his cards right, hopefully she will be wife number two and stick around longer than wife number one. He saw his mother put her phone away, her napkin down, and appeared ready to get out there and solve a crime. So he sipped the last of his tea, paid the waitress, and then got up from his chair.

"Ready, come on let's go solve a crime," joked Bob.

Chapter Eighteen

Mark went to work hung over as usual. He had such a headache. His boss was driving him crazy, so what if he was a little late, he'd work through lunch. No sense in taking a lunch break anyway if you have no one to meet up with for a little afternoon fooling around. He felt that sitting in the truck during noon time alone would drive him nuttier than he already was. So he sat in the grassy area nearby, with some of the other workers.

"You stink man," groaned a fellow worker, "don't you ever bath?"

"Go to hell," moaned Mark, "I was sick this morning, flu stuff."

"Well, you're drinking yourself sick," observed another worker.

Mark was a mess, and he knew it. He was angry. He was just an angry guy. He hated women but couldn't live without one. Maybe he could get Ellen back. Mark felt weird about killing Sally. At first, he didn't know what to feel. So he drank his feelings. He got a little more nervous when he saw the article in the newspaper about the car accident near the airport where they found the woman driver dead.

"Hey, let me see your paper when your done okay?"

"What, the sports?"

"No, that other section," Mark pointed. The guy nodded indicating to go ahead, take it, and Mark took the paper and walked over to lean against a truck fender to read it.

"Well, I'll be damn," he said out loud to himself. He began to feel a nervous twitch in his gut. Mark was nervous now, reading that the accident was being investigated.

"Come on men, time to get to work," his foreman yelled.

Mark quickly folded up the newspaper section he held and stuffed it in the back pocket of his work pants and went to join the other workers.

Chapter Nineteen

Bob and Laura drove out to the scene of the accident. They drove north on the black top service road until they saw tire skid marks leading into the ditch on the left side of the road.

"See those tire marks leading to the ditch," pointed out Bob.

"Yes, and that's a pretty deep ditch," exclaimed Laura, "and that is where the ditch is the deepest along this road."

"Yeah, and it's on a straightaway on the road," Bob pointed out, "so it is odd she would have a single car accident on the straightaway."

"And according to the tracks, the car landed almost perfectly perpendicular to the ditch," exclaimed Laura, "that would take some effort to steer the car to go directly in that ditch like that. It almost looks deliberate, doesn't it?"

"I agree," sighed Bob, "that alone makes the accident look suspiciously deliberate.

"If she fell asleep or passed out," said Laura, "I'm sure she would have driven into the deep ditch more at an angle, don't you think?"

"Yeah, this looks like she deliberately made a very sharp left turn into the ditch from the right lane as she was heading north."

"And where exactly does this road lead?" Laura wondered.

"Just about another mile to that neighborhood past those high powered utility lines . Just beyond that, I see the MetroLink station," reported Bob as he looked through binoculars he grabbed from the back seat of his car.

"So, let's check out the wooded area where the rug was found," suggested Laura.

Bob and Laura walked a bit away from where the car went into the ditch. They looked for footprints and particles of any evidence. They found work shoe type sole prints in the soft soil along the paved road that led to a weedy field near a wooded area. Then they saw the yellow tape marking the area where the crime scene crew removed the rug.

"Well, this is all very interesting," sighed Laura, "you have forms and pictures of the shoe prints, correct?"

"Yes, we do," reported Bob. There was enough evidence here to bring in the perpetrator. Laura and Bob thought the young woman died somewhere else, was wrapped in an area rug, then thrown in the trunk of her own car, and driven out here in hopes of staging a fatal accident. The scene was set to appear she may have been killed crashing her car into the ditch, or had a stroke or passed out, and then crashed her car in the ditch, hit her head and died. If there was indeed foul play and the perpetrator drove her body to that location and made it look like an accident, then that person could have easily walked over to the MetroLink station and rode the train to just about anywhere, even back home. How convenient. They wrapped up their visit to the accident scene and got ready to leave.

"Okay, well this was all very exciting," exclaimed Laura, "giving her son a quick hug. "It's grand to be out in the field again like I used to ride along with your father."

"I loved it Mom, we'll do more of this," replied Bob.

On the ride back to Laura's condo, they chatted about the case and were sure there was enough evidence to prove foul play. Now they just had to connect the dots, where was she murdered, and why, and then go after the perpetrator who did it.

"Want to come in?" asked Laura when they pulled up at her condo complex.

"No, wish I could," smiled Bob, I need to be back to the office to do some paperwork. We'll talk soon, okay? Love you, Mom." Bob waved good-bye and watched his mother as she entered her condo.

Chapter Twenty

"Hi," Ellen said from the kitchen as she poured herself a glass of iced tea. She was happy to see her friend.

"Want a glass of tea?"

"Sure, I'll have a glass," Laura was glad to see that Ellen was home.

"Nice to have you home early," Laura smiled.

"Yes, training ended a little early today, which was nice."

"How is it going," asked Laura, "do you think you will like working there?"

"I love it," replied Ellen, "it's tough, mostly you just have to be on your toes and pay attention not to miss any items in orders, and to pack things well. But it is so wonderful to feel alive and amongst the living, again. Having been married to that man for years was definitely, not "just a walk in the park", as the saying goes. All that mind control after a while just takes you down, and you totally lose yourself. You lose who you really are in this world. I had totally handed myself over to his mind control, not even realizing it. The manipulation and control come on so gradually that you do not even know it is happening. After a while you are just a shell of a person, a mere puppet, a voiceless mime merely preforming tricks for him. Slowly he had turned me into a battered, mindless, robotic slave. And I had no idea what was actually happening to me. I was numb. I think journaling and riding my bike every day helped to save my sanity."

"You poor thing," Laura said as she hugged her. "I can't imagine having to live like that."

They both turned and laughed through tears as they saw Emma standing behind them with her leash in her mouth, a smile in her eyes, and her little stump of a tail wagging her whole butt. As if Emma knew what they needed, she knew how to break the sadness she saw. Emma decided it was time to get the ladies out for a lovely walk in the park. It was evening, a delightful time of the day, and the birds were singing their last songs of the day. The setting sun, casted a shimmering glow on the trees, and the grass and lit up the Art Museum's giant stone structure with a golden glow. Ducks were swimming and paddle boat paddlers were steering back to the Boathouse. Some would enjoy a lovely candlelight, lake-side dinner with a relaxing glass of wine, entertained by a classical string quartet. And all of that made for a beautiful evening on the restaurant patio.

"I love the Boathouse," sighed Laura as they walked

near it on the walkway past the 1902 Worlds' Fair Pavilion.

"It looks wonderful."

"What do you say, we have dinner here in celebration of your new job, on me," suggested Laura., "I want to celebrate."

"Oh wow, that is so sweet of you. You have done so much for me already, letting me stay with you, loaning me the money for a down payment on my car."

"I am only too happy to help, it's just a walk in the park." Laura smiled as she led Ellen and Emma across the street toward the restaurant.

"I see you picked up on my saying," Ellen teased. She always said "it's just a walk in the park" to herself when trying to cope and get through the worst of times. She did not realize just how often she had the chance to use it to psych herself up and convince herself that all would be well, one more time.

They walked up to the entrance and asked if Emma could come in and lay down by the table if they ate on the patio. The hostess was the manager's daughter and proud owner of a Rottweiler herself. So she was more than willing to accommodate Emma. She made special arrangements just for them, seating them at a table off to the side of the patio, where it was more private. And of course, Emma knew to be her best self. She followed the hostess along with the ladies and walked gingerly minding her own business. She dared not stop to sniff anything, and when the kind hostess seated the ladies, she gave the sweet Rottweiler a big hug. . The restaurant was not busy right then, so the young hostess knew she wouldn't get in trouble with her manager father.

"Here's to your new job," Laura said as they clinked wine glasses in a toast.

"You're the best," Ellen's teary eyes shined in the candlelight, "thank you."

They enjoyed a loving dinner of salad greens, charbroiled lemon chicken, and roasted vegetables. When the waitress asked if they wanted desert. They did indeed but were too full and decided to have desert at home. They declined the desert offer, and decided they needed the walk to to make room for the ice cream that awaited them at home.

The sun had set. It was dark, but the full moon lit their way. They could see well enough, so instead of walking along the street on the sidewalk, they chose to walk on the paved path through the park, from the Boathouse toward Art Hill where the Shakespeare outdoor plays were held every year, and then toward Skinker Blvd. where they would cross over to Laura's condo.

There was light traffic in the park and headlights would come upon them and then pass as they trekked down Art Hill. For some odd reason Laura, felt an uneasy feeling. Her intuition was telling her something was off. Suddenly Laura had the urge to take Ellen's elbow and lead her to the right, off from the sidewalk. She quickly followed Emma who led them behind some bushes. Ellen thought Emma had to potty. But Laura sensed that Emma had the same instincts she did, to get off the sidewalk away from the street. Within seconds,

92

they got behind some large cedar shrubbery, and they were glad that they did, for they heard a large vehicle coming up the street behind them. With the help of the light of the full moon, they saw a big red pickup with dual rear wheels adorned with naked lady mud flaps reflecting the light from the streetlamps. The truck passed very slowly as if the driver was searching for someone.

"Oh, that was him," Ellen said frightened. "Holy crap, that was close."

"I had a feeling" declared Laura, "I think Emma had the same feeling because she led me, rather pulled me actually, off the sidewalk so we would be behind those bushes. I think she knew danger was approaching because she hasn't gone potty yet. Oh, okay, there she goes, okay."

"I'm shaking," sighed Ellen, "I am even more afraid of him now, since those divorce papers were served. He must be really mad. What am I going to do? He's refusing to sign them the lawyer said."

Laura and Ellen decided to stay off the sidewalk and wait and watch a bit. After a minute, they crept further out on the sidewalk to see if by chance which direction the truck was headed. They saw him turn left to go out of the park and then turn right to go north on Skinker Boulevard, away from the direction of Laura's condo. They were glad to see he was heading the opposite way from Laura's condo. They did not poke around. Emma appeared also to be ready to get back home, as she quickly did her business. Laura, Ellen and Emma cut across the grass toward the path, and hurriedly crossed Skinker Boulevard at the cross walk. Finally, they were home and happy to be inside.

They were glad to be back home safe and sound and to the treat of two pints of Ben and Jerry's Cherry Garcia in the freezer. Two scoops of ice cream and a cup of decaf coffee helped soothe their nerves. They sat on the couch and enjoyed every bite, as they talked over the day's events.

"You know Laura," sighed Ellen, "I just realized, I can be putting you and Emma in danger. That man is crazy!"

"Oh, not to worry," assured Laura, "it's just a walk in the park. I'll ask my archangels to protect us."

"No, really," Ellen said, "I feel bad."

"I think we'll be okay," Laura replied, "besides we have our guard dog Emma."

Hearing her name, Emma lying on the rug at their feet, raised her head up a bit and cocked it ever so slightly. Emma looked at Laura, then at the ice cream, then back at Laura as if to say, "I'm ready for mine."

"No, Emma, I was not offering you ice cream," Laura got up and got Emma a treat from her treat jar on the kitchen counter. Emma was happy.

"No really, I mean it," protested Ellen, "the man is crazy."

"It's okay, I love having you here," Laura got back to their conversation as she sat down on the couch.

"I certainly appreciate you," Ellen said. They both were happy about their arrangement and just left it there as it was, for now. Laura wanted to talk about other things, like her day with her son.

"So, while you were at work today…" Laura said patting Ellen's knee being all proud of herself. "I was with my son, working on a case with him, just like I used to do with his father. We had a grand day."

"So what case were you working on?"

"Oh, the one where they found the deceased young woman in the car, that ran into the ditch, out near the airport."

"Oh, tell me more," pleaded Ellen.

Laura proceeded to give Ellen the details. How they drove to the evidence lot and found and retrieved cloth fibers from the trunk. She told Ellen how they found hair fibers and fingerprints in the car. She told Ellen about the nice lunch, and the drive to the crash scene where they looked around and found what appeared to be men's work shoe prints in the soft ground near where the rug was stashed. The evidence was now stored in the evidence locker. It was confirmed that the rug that was found under the brush in a wooded area near the accident scene matched fibers found in the trunk of the car. Laura saw that Ellen was interested, so pulled out her iPhone and prepared to show Ellen pictures she had taken.

"See we took pictures of the trunk, inside and around the car." Laura showed Ellen.

"Yes, and that is the car we thought looked so oddly familiar," stated Ellen staring at the picture.

"Look at this," said Laura as she noticed the pictures

were the ones they took the day they followed Mark to his work site. It dawned on them both at the same time. It was the day they had taken pictures of a young blonde woman getting out of an old Chevy with dented multi-colored doors who got into Mark's unlocked truck. Evidently, they had plans for her to meet him there for their lunch time rendezvous.

Ellen's eyes grew big, "That car definitely looks like the one in the picture you took the day we followed Mark to work."

"Yes, it certainly does, doesn't it," agreed Laura.

"Amazing," Ellen said, and they looked at each other. In that moment they knew what had happened to that girl.

"Let's look at more pictures," suggested Laura. She went back to the pictures they took at the scene and the evidence they found.

"There's a picture of the rug?" asked Ellen.

"Yes, when they opened it up and rolled it out, they matched blood stains with the woman's blood, and the fibers of the rug matched the fibers found in the trunk of the car she was found in.

"Let's look at that picture of the rug rolled out," suggested Ellen. Laura got it back and spread it out with her fingers on the screen to make the pattern and color of the rug appear larger so they could see it better.

"That's the rug that was under the coffee table and two recliners in the living room of our house," Ellen said with a positive tone. She was certain it was the same rug.

"Hm, if you have no pictures of that rug in your house, we can never prove that it was ever in your house. So, we would have to try to match cloth fibers left behind. And while we are there, we could try to match hair and other fiber samples."

The ladies made plans to try to find a photo of Laura's house that may have the area rug in the picture. But thought that would be unlikely. The better bet was to try to match hair and fiber samples. They needed to get to Mark and Laura's house to collect those samples. They both dreaded having to do that.

Chapter Twenty-One

Mark looked pretty rough, even the guys on his work crew noticed it. He just said he wasn't sleeping well lately. After work at the bar, guys from work never learned much about Mark. He mostly listened, made a few comments once in a while, laughed along with the others, and for sure drank more than anyone else there. Mark had something that haunted him now, a big secret. Over and over in his head he kept hearing the word, murderer. He was not a murderer he reasoned, as it was all Ellen's fault. She drove him to this by leaving him. He vowed to find Ellen and teach her a lesson for leaving him and serving him divorce papers.

Mark had the notion that a wife was property; so therefore, Ellen was his property. Ellen was his own personal punching bag when the boss made him mad at work, can't hit the boss, so take your frustrations out on your wife. He also got on her when she didn't cook his food right, the way he liked it, or do his laundry right, the way he liked his shirts ironed. He was determined to find her and drag her back home if need be. So when he was not at work, he drove around the park looking for her on her bike because he knew she rode her bike around the park paths. He was going to find her and drag her by her hair back home. The bitch was his. Mark grew up with a wife beating father and that was how he learned his asinine behavior. The real truth was Mark was very insecure and afraid of being left alone and so he drank to numb his feelings.

Mark was always hungover, and so wasn't a good worker and he knew it. Many times the guys on the crew had to come back around and redo his framing before pouring concrete. But still he persevered and showed up everyday, hungover or not. In his own strange way, Mark missed Sally too. Especially at lunch time when he walked to his truck, and she was not there waiting for him.

Chapter Twenty-Two

Mark missed Sally, so at lunch he drove to McDonald's on Hampton Avenue, that was where she had worked and that was where they had begun chatting it up at the drive-through window, when he placed his orders. Now and then she threw in an extra burger, or an extra-large order of fries for him. But now when he pulled up to the window, she wasn't there. Sally's friend Missy was working that window now. So, he went after her. He would be extra nice. He asked what shift Sally was working these days, and Missy looked sad.

"Man, don't you read the papers," groaned Missy, she was short of patience that day. Seems everyone was asking about Sally. "Sally died in a car accident."

"Oh my gosh, I am so sorry to hear that," grimaced Mark, as if he didn't know, "I really liked Sally. How tragic." He tried his best to sound surprised and sad at the same time.

"Yeah, I miss my friend," Missy said fighting back tears.

"Well, when do you get off work, maybe we can grab a coffee or a beer," suggested Mark to pretty little red-headed Missy. He thought she looked so sad, he wanted to cheer her up, but actually he just wanted to win over another potential victim. Mark wondered if Missy was another run-away like Sally without family or anyone to be concerned about her. In other words, an easy target, to be used and abused and never missed when he got tired of her and then disposed of her.

"I came in early so I get off at three today," answered Missy. She figured Mark was an okay guy. Anyway, Sally always liked him. So why not and talking with a mutual friend about Sally might help her overcome her sadness of losing her best friend and co-worker.

"Great, I'll come by here when I get off work at three and pick you up. Think about where you want to have that beer."

Mark was at McDonald's on Hampton Avenue to pick up Missy a little after three. He saw her sitting at one of the outside tables when he pulled up. He reached over and pushed open the passenger-side truck door. Missy easily climbed up into the big red truck. She was impressed by this powerful man with his shiny new truck. Sally had told her that Mark worked in construction and made lots of money. Missy thought *why not give him a try*, and although he was a lot older than, Tony, her current boyfriend, she didn't care. She could use a boyfriend who made good money. So what if he was a bit older than Tony, who worked at Lowe's. Tony was about Missy's age. He was cute enough, nice enough, slender enough. But he appeared weak to Missy and just wasn't manly enough for her. She thought of him as more of a mama's boy. And to Missy manly meant a tall, strong with rugged looks; but most importantly made good money.

"How about Duke's in the Central West End, think that would be nice," suggested Mark. He knew he could be nice when he wanted, especially when encircling pretty prey.

"Sure, that sounds fine," said Missy has they headed to the Central West End.

Mark was actually lucky to find a parking spot right on the street on Lucid near the Left Bank Books store. Mark had a change of clothes in his truck and so had quickly changed out of his dirty work clothes when he got off work. He had on a nice pair of jeans and wore a untucked light blue long-sleeve shirt. He knew how to dress to impress the ladies. He also liked wearing his cowboy boots that made him look more slim and taller still. He admired his physique in the reflections of the store front windows as he and Missy strolled down the sidewalk toward Duke's. He thought Missy complemented him as she looked cute in her pink tank top, skinny jeans and sandals. They sat at a corner table in the bar room. Mark thought she looked hungry, even thou she's smelled of French fries, the telltale clues of working at McDonald's for hours. Missy never minded the smell anymore, she got used to smelling like an order of hamburger and fries. She thought the smell of enticing French fries probably made Mark feel hungry too.

"Are you hungry," asked Mark, "want to get something to eat?"

The waiter brought over two menus with their frosty mugs of Bud Lite draft beer. Missy was hungry and wanted anything besides a hamburger and fries. She ordered the grilled Salmon with sautéed oven-roasted root vegetables. Mark ordered the prime rib with loaded baked potato. When the food was delivered to their table, Mark ordered two more mugs of beer. Mark was having fun as was Missy. They enjoyed their dinners.

"So where are you living Missy?" Mark asked.

"With a friend from work in her apartment," revealed Missy. Her intuition told her to leave it at that. She was glad when Mark than changed the subject.

"Hey, want to take in a movie this evening?" suggested Mark. "Maybe something at the Chase or Hi Pointe, let's look online," and he got out his cell phone to check as did she. They decided on a thriller at the Chase movie theatre.

"I need to stop by home first, I live in the De Mun Boulevard area, is that okay with you?" asked Mark. He really did not want to waste time seeing a stupid movie. He wanted to get her back at his place, for some sex fun.

"Sure, that's fine," replied Missy.

"Great," said Mark, "I need to check on something I might have left turned on. I just want to make sure, since I have not been home all day."

It was a fairly short drive from the Central West End to his house near Clayton Road and De Mun Avenue. They chitchatted about this and that and the weather along the way. They were both feeling the beers they drank.

Mark pulled into his driveway. He had a nice big house and was proud of it.

"Come on in," suggested Mark, "I will show you my place. I've been thinking about knocking down a wall and remodeling the kitchen and living room to make it an open space. Say, maybe you can give me some ideas." Mark knew this approach was his best yet. He had her in the palm of his hand.

"Sure," Missy was most agreeable. So far, she liked Mark. He was tall and strong. She felt safe with him, unlike her stupid, timid boyfriend, Tony, who she had been dating.

"How about a beer," Mark offered when they entered the side door and she followed him into the kitchen as he headed for the refrigerator.

"Okay," smiled Missy as he handed the beer bottle to her. The bottle felt good in her hands. It was nice and cold right out of the refrigerator and felt good going down her dry parched throat. She had a slight buzz going already after the two beers at Duke's. Mark got himself another beer, too.

He took his time and showed her around the house and shared his remodeling ideas. She thought some were a great idea, like knocking down a non-weight-bearing wall that separated the living room from the kitchen. He wanted to create an open floor plan with a kitchen counter snack bar that would separate the two rooms. He liked the idea of an open floor plan kitchen and living room. He thought that way, he could cook and easily watch the television in the living room, or visit with his lady sitting at the snack bar counter while she watched him cook. Missy agreed and also thought that an open floor plan was a good idea.

"I need to go to the basement to check on that blower I was concerned about," Mark informed her.

"Okay," Missy was most agreeable enjoying the cold beer and feeling the calming light-headed effects of it.

"Come, I'll show you my work shop I have in the basement," invited Mark, "I am very proud of it, just got some new tools. I plan on doing the remodeling myself. Mark was proud of his idea of woodworking and remodeling talents.

Missy didn't mind him going on and on about himself, she liked him well enough, she thought. And her friend Sally had always said good things about Mark, so she trusted him. She thought if she played her cards right, that Mark would like her too. She thought it would be great to live in this house. Maybe she could even get a car one day. Maybe she could stop having to work at McDonald's, maybe even get married to a guy who makes good money, like Mark. Missy wanted to be taken care of, what young woman doesn't want a good strong man to support her and take care of her. She thought he would fit in and was just right for all her friends. They all had the same mind-set, wanting a boyfriend and then get married and possibly have a family. As he led her to the basement, she lived in her daydreaming thoughts and acted interested to learn about his woodworking skills.

It was dark in the basement, lit only by a single pull-chain light bulb. Mark pulled the chain and switched it on. It was dim. Mark had Missy right where he wanted her. He was enjoying himself.

Mark liked the idea of having her cornered, under his power. Just like he had with Sally. He had power over Missy now. He could do what he wanted and that excited him. Missy could be his new sex slave. He suddenly had the urge to kiss her.

"Its dark down here," expressed Missy stumbling and nearly tripping over a garden hose curled up on the concrete floor.

"Come, over here, I'll show you my workshop," invited Mark. Oh, he was getting excited now. His heart was racing. He wanted to kiss her.

Missy never saw him go and check anything like the blower, that he said he was going to check down in the basement. She did not say anything, but this made her a bit nervous. After all, it was the reason he said he had to go home and down in the basement in the first place. She wasn't interested in seeing his tools, or his workshop. The single bulb, pull-chain, ceiling light may have been dim, but not too dim for Missy to see the sudden sick hungry look in Mark's eyes. She suddenly wanted to leave, as she was beginning to feel cornered. She backed toward the steps a bit. He noticed.

"Hey, come here, I want to show you this," pleaded Mark as if he was so harmless as not to hurt a baby lamb like her.

"I have to get going," Missy stammered, then she remembered she had no car, he picked her up from work. She would have to sneak away and walk home. She figured it was about three miles. She could take short cuts so it wouldn't be too bad to walk. She walked about that same distance every day to work, so she was used to walking a lot.

"Why, we're just getting acquainted," Mark said with beer breath moving in closer. Her increased nervousness was a turn-on for him. Then he remembered how Sally had struggled, how that was a true turn-on, he wanted more of that feeling; that conquering feeling. He blocked her move, by stepping between her and the steps leading up to the main floor of the house.

"I have to get going," demanded Missy quickly moving sideways in hopes to slip past him.

"No, you don't" Mark replied showing a foul mouth with missing teeth as he faced her and held her by the shoulders. Missy never noticed his sad looking teeth before. It was a real turn-off. Regretfully, she was beginning to realize she had been living in a dream world where she created an image of Mark to suit her own taste and needs. Now for the first time she was beginning to see the real Mark and how he truly was. Suddenly, she wondered about Sally. Did he kill Sally then stage an auto accident to cover it up?

Realizing that possibility sprang Missy into panic

mode. She wiggled and twisted and broke from his grasp and fought her way up the basement steps. He was right behind her and tried to grab her ankle. He kept trying, kept missing, and finally succeeded. But she would have none of it. She twisted her ankle right out of his grasp and then managed to turn enough to give Mark a good swift kick to his face right on the nose. When she reached the top of the steps, she turned around and saw the evil look in his eyes and his ugly shinny sweating face. The light from the kitchen illuminated his face, it frightened her. She could see his booze swollen face lined with wrinkles, surrounding his scary, piercing, evil red blood-shot eyes. What was she thinking? She had to be nuts to go out with this maniac. He tried to grab her again. She again twisted out of his grasp. And when he slightly lost his balance, she took advantage of the opportunity of his sudden vulnerability, and gave him another swift kick with the back of her heel, this time right in his groin. She smiled as he doubled over with pain losing his balance and falling down a few steps until he managed to grab on to the banister railing.

He was fighting mad now after being kicked again and losing his balance. Enjoying her moment of triumph and getting a little revenge, Missy turned a bit to face him and gave him another good kick to the face as he came up behind her. This time he fell backwards to the basement floor. Missy did not hang around to see if he was alive or dead. She was out of there. She slammed the basement door shut, quickly slide over the latch lock, and turned the dead bolt into the lock position. She wanted to secure the door and quickly grabbed a kitchen chair, it was heavy oak wood, and slide it over and managed to prop the chair at an angle under the doorknob. It fit snugly, and she was pleased. Not hearing anything from the basement, she mentally slowed down her anxieties a bit and her fears lightened up.

He wouldn't be charging up the basement steps after her, she knew he was either unconscious or dead. She had time to rethink her plan. She was afraid and wanted to make sure he could not get to her. She decided to add the kitchen table as another barricade against the basement door, as it would fit perfectly over the angled chair tucked under the doorknob. She pulled the heavy kitchen table with all her might. Evidently it was one of Mark woodworking projects as it was ornately carved made of solid oak. She struggled but managed to pull, then got behind it and pushed the kitchen table over in front of the basement door to block it from opening.

She had no idea why she did it, but she then had the urge to wrap her fingerprints off everything. She merely guessed she had watched too many crime shows on television to get that idea. But she thought at the time it was a good idea. She grabbed the kitchen towel and wiped down every surface she thought she may have touched. It took a few minutes and in those few minutes she thought she was beginning to hear rumblings from the basement. Evidently he wasn't unconscious or dead but on the move. She had to get out of there and fast.

She ran out the back door, past his truck parked in the driveway and ran out onto the street. She didn't notice the silver Prius with two women sitting in it until it was right in front of her, and she almost ran smack into it.

Chapter Twenty-Three

Ellen and Laura had just come back from walking Emma and decided to run some errands. They left Emma at home because they had several stops to make. They went to shop at Sam's to get a few things, and then they went grocery shopping at Dierburgs. After they left the grocery store, a spark of intuition led Laura to drive pass Ellen's house.

"I want to take a drive past your house now," said Laura.

"Okay, I'll prepare myself. I hate the thought of going there and Mark being there."

"I'll make it quick," said Laura, "I just have the feeling something is off."

Laura had a feeling something wasn't quite right. So they drove to Ellen's house and parked down from it on the street. They saw Mark's truck in the driveway and thought they would sit for a few minutes and watch and wait. Laura had to play out her intuition.

"We probably should have taken our groceries home

first," thought Ellen, "but I think it should be okay, we didn't buy ice cream this time."

"Let's just sit here for a minute or two," suggested Laura. "I'm getting something." By that Laura meant that she was sensing something. She had an intuitive feeling that something wasn't right. That perhaps someone was in trouble.

"It's getting dark, we're not going to see too much for long," thought Ellen.

"What's that," asked Laura suddenly seeing some movement from the driveway near Mark's truck.

"Is that a woman running from the house?" asked Ellen. "I think she came out the side door."

"Yes, I see her too," declared Laura. She had the sudden urge then to step on the gas pedal and move up closer. She got to the edge of the driveway when the woman ran into the street in front of her car; practically running into Laura's car. Laura would have hit her if she didn't suddenly hit the brakes. Laura saw that the young woman looked frazzled and frightened and very upset. So Laura quickly lowered her driver-side window to speak to the woman.

"Hurry, get in the back seat," Laura hollered at her, "it's unlocked, just get in." She stuck her head out the window ordering the frightened young woman to get into the car.

"Oh my gosh, that man is crazy," cried Missy as she took Laura up on her offer and hurriedly slide into the back seat. In one quick motion she slid in and moved the grocery bags over making more room for herself.

"Let's get out of here," ordered Ellen in a strained voice. "Come on, let's get out of here." Ellen was afraid Mark would be running out of the house chasing after the girl. She did not want Mark to see her and possibly recognize her in the car, so Laura hurried and sped away.

Laura and Ellen quickly introduced themselves to Missy, and she to them as they drove out of the neighborhood. Missy told them that she was a friend of Sally's, the young woman who just passed in a car accident out near the airport. The ladies looked at each other with a mutual knowing glance. They said they saw that piece about the car accident in the newspaper.

Missy did not say anything to the ladies about Mark falling down the basement steps and how she barricaded the basement door with him down there.

"You'll be safe now," Ellen tried to console Missy.

"Sally was my friend and co-worker at McDonald's, the one on Hampton closest to the park," stated Missy.

"So you knew Sally," confirmed Laura.

"I knew that Sally was seeing a guy who worked in construction. I knew she would go to his work site at lunch before coming to work to start her shift. She told me all about Mark. She met Mark when he came through the drive-thru window. They got chummy. She started seeing him. Sally came from nothing, and she liked the idea that Mark was a construction worker, drove a big new shinny truck, and figured he made good money. She just wanted to get married and have a man take care of her."

"Well, Mark certainly wasn't a good pick if you are looking for someone to treat you right." Ellen sadly informed Missy. "I'm his wife by the way."

"Oh gosh, sorry I did not realize he was married," stated Missy, "but I guess I could have figured as much. Every man I meet seems to be married."

"We can drive you to your home," suggested Laura, "does Mark know where you live?"

"No, he just knows I work at that McDonald's on Hampton."

"Well, be prepared, he may be stalking and harassing you now while you are at work, and since it is a public place, it will be hard to stop him."

The ladies decided while they still had Missy with them, to question her more about Sally and her habits.

"Missy, do you have any idea why Sally would have been driving out near the airport the night of her auto accident?" asked Laura.

"I can't think of any reason Sally would be driving toward the airport," Missy replied. "She actually lived near me in a house with other fast food restaurant workers who worked in the area."

"So, in your opinion, Missy," asked Laura, "what do you think really happened to Sally?"

"Well, after my own personal experience with idiot Mark," said Missy, "I think he tried to tie her up, keep her in the basement. They struggled, and maybe she hit her head. Anyway, she died, or he flat out killed her, then he staged her car to make it look like her death was caused by crashing her car in the ditch."

"Well, between you and us," revealed Ellen, "we share your same sentiment and thoughts about how and why the crime took place.

Chapter Twenty-Four

Mark was infuriated that he had to chop his way out of his own basement. But getting out of the locked basement was no problem for Mark. He had all kinds of tools in his workshop in the basement. He had everything he needed. He had several power saws, drills and bits, crow bars, even a pickaxe. So he got out in record time. Of course, he was angry that in order to break out, he had to ruin the basement door, the kitchen table and chair he designed and built himself. He cursed her with every whack of the axe, and pry of the crowbar. When he finally managed to shove the chair and table out of the way, he ran outside to the edge of the driveway and looked in both directions but did see not her. He figured by the time it took him to cut and smash his way out of his basement prison, she would be long gone.

It was as if she just disappeared into the night. He figured she just flagged down a car. No problem if she got away from him this time. It just made the game a little more exciting. There was always next time, as he knew where she worked. She was nothing but a tramp anyway. Probably just another run-away whore who would never be missed--another reason why she was curious prey to him.

Chapter Twenty-Five

Laura and Ellen drove Missy home to the apartment she shared with two other McDonald's co-workers. It was close enough to work that she could walk to and from work, which she did every day.

The ladies got Missy's contact information. Laura encouraged Missy to keep her eyes and ears open and to stay away from Mark because he could be a very dangerous man. After her terrifying experience, Missy had learned her lesson and readily vowed to be careful. She realized that she could have gotten herself in the same fix as Sally, if she wasn't careful, and she knew this as every fiber of her being told her so. The ladies asked Missy to keep in touch, and Missy told the ladies she would testify in court if it ever came to that. After Missy got out of the car at her apartment, Ellen and Laura continued talking about the situation with Mark as they drove home.

"Mark needs to be arrested and taken off the streets," insisted Ellen, "this can't keep happening."

"Tomorrow morning bright and early I'll call Bob and see if we can make arrangements to get together and talk about this," Laura promised.

Most days, Missy did see Mark in his big red pickup truck parked in the corner of the McDonald's parking lot where he could sit and watch her work at her drive-through window. He could practically watch her every move. She could feel him staring at her, it was most unnerving. And she knew it was him because could see him in the truck, and when he pulled in and backed around, she could see those unmistakable dual rear wheels that were horribly adorned with those outrageous naked lady mud flaps. Missy noticed that most days he parked in the corner of the parking lot and just sat there and stared at the drive-through window where she worked. It was obvious to her that he was trying to let her know that he was watching her and spying on her every move. Or worse yet, he would place an order at the drive-thru window in hopes she was working that window. Missy always managed to grab another co-worker and trade spots for a second when she saw that he was coming through the line where she was working. Her co-workers were most cooperative as many of them have had the same experiences and readily understood her predicament.

Chapter Twenty-Six

Ellen was off work the next day, so Ellen and Laura set a time to visit with Bob at his office at Police Headquarters. They talked about Mark's possible ties to Sally Adams' death and told Bob about Missy's close call with Mark. Ellen could not understand why the police just couldn't arrest Mark on suspicion of homicide involving Sally Adams' death and just search his house. Ellen and Laura were sure that the fibers and hair samples they had collected of Sally's would match any samples found in Mark and Ellen's house. Bob assured the ladies that he and his fellow detectives were working on it as best as he could, but there were many other cases to be solved. He explained that the department's case load was backlogged. He apologized profusely to the ladies.

"It's just that the department is so busy right now. We can't keep up, our case load is at a record high," explained Bob. He was sorry that things could not be moved along faster. "We are backed up as we are short of personnel due to several recent retirements."

"Well, we appreciate anything you can do to get this dangerous man off the streets so I can move on with my life," expressed Ellen.

After they left Bob's office the ladies decided they needed a treat. They drove to Ted Drew's on Chippewa and got frozen yogurt and ice cream and sat outside at a picnic table in the warm sunshine to enjoy their yummy treats. Ellen chose delicious peach yogurt, and Laura thought about going to her go-to favorite, dark chocolate with cherry and nut toppings. But she always had to stand and debate with herself because it was always a toss-up between dark chocolate and butter pecan ice cream. They both got a good laugh out of not being able to make up their minds, because it all looked so delicious. They both ended up getting two different favored scoops of ice cream in a dish. They carried on with oohs and aah with each spoonful that melted in their mouths. They were wonderful treats that took their minds off of a very bad person if only for a few delicious moments.

Chapter Twenty-Seven

Everything was going fairly well for Missy she walked to work every day. Missy had not seen the big red pick-up truck sitting in the parking lot at McDonald's for several days now, and that worried her. She wondered what Mark was up to though. She hoped that horrible Mark had just given up and gone away.

She still cautiously walked home taking different routes on different streets, always looking over her shoulder, sometimes she even cut through people's yards, to get to her apartment. If it was daylight or dark, and she thought she saw a big red pick-up truck approaching in a distance, she would quickly cut through yards, hide behind trees or vehicles, just whatever it took to get out of his range of sight during daylight hours, or what headlight beams provided at night.

It was nerve-racking having to do this every day. She chose to work different shifts, so her hours were varied and not routine, which she was grateful to be able to do.

Her hours were so varied she could not keep up with her schedule herself, so she hoped it confused Mark as well, and that he would just give up and stay away. But that wasn't the case.

The work shifts Missy dreaded the most were the ones where she got off work when it was late and she had to walk home in the dark. All he had to do was sit parked near her work, then when he saw her leave, follow her home. Missy was always cautious, so when it was time to get off of work, she always checked to see if the coast was clear. If she saw his truck in the parking lot, she would have to sneak out another exit and circle around to keep out of sight.

Chapter Twenty-Eight

"Damn, that little shit got away," Mark was drunk, tired and angry. Mostly he was just plain angry. The audacity of that little bitch locking him in his own basement and barricading the basement door with his priceless home built handcrafted kitchen table and chair set. It really infuriated him. It infuriated him that she got the best of him and that he had to trash the door, a chair and the kitchen table, but mostly because she got the upper hand. He had thoroughly ruined the basement door and the kitchen table and chair by hacking and sawing his way out of the basement.

He was mad as hell and swore that Little Miss Missy would have to pay for the damages she caused him and his property. He was mad and ready to have a little fun scaring the living daylights out of her. She deserved it for pulling one over on him. Well, he knew where she worked which put his mind at ease. He slept through the nights, woke up and went to work each morning. He had drunken hang-over headaches that were out of this world and that aspirins did not help, and that made him even more angry.

Without fail, every day after he got off work Mark drove to where Missy worked. He was not through with her yet. Finally, after a week or more, he spotted her in the distance crossing the street walking away from McDonald's. He slowly pulled his truck out of the McDonald's parking lot and followed her. He drove very slowly, which was a sheer dead give-away that it was him headed up the street.

But before Missy ever saw his creeping truck coming down the street, she sensed him. She felt his evil energy enveloping her surroundings. She was scared but becoming more angry than anything. She was getting tired of having to be frightened every day by some idiot maniac. Why should she have to tolerate an idiot like this.

She had begun carrying a knife with her. She borrowed a nice sharp knife from McDonald's for her own on and off the job personal security, so she justified her reasoning. She wasn't stealing, she told herself, she was borrowing and would return it the next day; of course, she said that every day. She figured working at such an exposed place like McDonald's, she had the right to any means to protect herself getting to and from her workplace. She carried the knife with its very sharp serrated blade in her hand. She was ready. Come and get me, she thought to herself.

Like the idiot Mark was, he slowly pulled up behind her. Yelled at her that he wanted to talk. She ignored him and kept on walking on the side of the street just as she was doing. She was determined to ignore him. Mark, who was determined not to be ignored, decided to stop the truck, get out and walk up to Missy to talk, so he swore to her.

"Missy, I just want to talk," cried Mark in his big baby voice as if he was so hurt and sorry for how he treated her. He was using his best pleading voice. Anyway, he thought it was his best sweet voice"

"Get lost, you loser," Missy growled. She had had enough. She might had said "get lost" but she was actually wishing for him to get closer, she was angry. She wanted him in range so she could punch his lights out. She wanted revenge, badly.

"Now, now," Mark sounded like he thought he was just a poor misunderstood lover.

"Beat it," she growled as she stepped up her pace a bit.

"I just want to talk," pleaded Mark a little out of breath. But he finally caught up to her and had the audacity to grab her elbow. Big mistake, he instantly realized.

Missy wasn't having any of it. She twisted her arm out of his grip and came around and stuck the knife she had hidden in her hand, into his arm, jabbing him. She laughed and mocked him when he screamed like a girl. His screaming angered her even more because Mr. Big Shot could dish it out, but he sure couldn't take it. Big baby, she thought. She wasn't finished yet, and as he cradled his bleeding arm, crying, she managed to get close enough to jab him in his thigh. She enjoyed the look of surprise in his blood-shot eyes as he doubled over. And then because she just could not resist, she took advantage of open target, and kicked him a good one right in the groin. Seeing him doubled over in severe pain, gave her great pleasure and a feeling of strength and independence. She could take care of herself. He remained lying there in a fetal position as she ran off into the night. She took short-cuts, detours, and crisscrossed streets. No way, did she want idiot Mark to learn where she was living, which would not only put herself in danger, but put her roommates in danger as well.

At one point, Missy turned back to look and watched Mark limp and struggle to get back into his truck. He finally drove off in the direction from which he came. She was glad he was hurting. She was proud for standing up for herself. And she hoped Mark finally received the message, that messing with Missy was going to be painful and hopefully remorseful; that is, if he even had a conscience.

Chapter Twenty-Nine

M issy wondered why some men were so evil, cold and calculus jerks. Missy read a lot in her spare time and watched the various interviews on *Open Minds* on GAIA TV. She was curious to learn why there were so many evil people in powerful positions around the world. She read the book, *Alien World Order*, by Len Kasten. She found out that Reptilians were on Draco then Orion then came to planet Earth and resided on Lemuria before humans were on Atlantis. The Reptilians on Lemuria harassed the humans living on Atlantis. The humans got tired of it and drove the Reptilians underground where they were very technical and built high-speed railways and underground cities.

Humans were better equipped with weapons to defend themselves against the Reptilians, so out-right war was not the answer to overrule the humans on Atlantis. So the Reptilians came up with the idea of creating Reptilian and human hybrids and shapeshifting to appear as human. And many of the hybrids were now on Earth's surface as shape-shifting hybrids infiltrated into positions of heads of corporations, banks, the medical community, and governments. They are without conscience and wish to depopulate and take over the planet once again.

Missy was becoming fearful just in general. She read where these Reptilian Hybrids claim Earth as their own and have resurfaced from the underground; they want their planet back and the humans gone. Call it Omega or Agenda21, the Great Reset, or the New World Order, but depopulation is the order of the day. She read Reptilian Hybrids had no soul or conscience. They cannot feel love or compassion for anyone as pure humans can. They are geared for provoking fear, conquest and takeover.

Missy wondered, was Mark a Reptilian hybrid? His eyes were shaped a little like Reptilian eyes, now that she thought about it. So, we are being attacked from within our own systems. Missy was depressed after reading that book, but believed all she read, because she saw it in everyday life in the form of toxic GMO (genetically modified organisms) foods, the side-effects of advertising and propaganda-based band-aided medical programs forced on to us involve toxic treatments, drugs, and vaccines. Missy read there are no cures, because to "cure" would mean the stopping and ending of the production of GMO foods and medicines with toxic side-effects. She read over one hundred thousand people die every year from taking prescription drugs as prescribed.

Medical doctors are taught not to use the word "cure." For to cure would mean prevention in the first place, which means growing only organic and cleaning up the environment, and building up everyone's immune system with sunshine, Vitamin D, and other supplements and grounding. And of course, lighten the load of stress and solve troubles and emotional problems that led to the illness in the first place. All of which for-profit modern day allopathic medicine does not do. Instead, they promote propaganda that leads to stress and fear which also lowered one's immune system defenses. A toxic combination when combined with fake food and the side-effects of medicines and vaccines strongly propagated by controlled media outputs. Our bodies are electrical, not chemical, she read.

Missy began to recognize the ill effects of the rule by a Reptilian patriarchal system in her everyday life. She saw it in the wars for land, oil and power, the racism, the degrading of women and molesting of children, and the drug and sex trades. It was clear to Missy that the Reptilians Hybrids were on the rise and taking action to kill humans off as they wanted to claim back their planet. The Reptilian Hybrids are in the process of thinning the herd. The plan was to depopulate the globe via war and famine and take it back from the humans. The only solution or the way to slow them down, she read, was by acts of kindness and love. Love was the only answer. Love was the only solution to conquering the evil, heartless, without conscience Reptilian Hybrids.

Missy thought of all the evil in the world, and it

saddened her as she walked the rest of her way to her apartment. She thought up more ways to deter Mark if he should choose to continue to harass her. Oh yeah, she planned to keep the knife handy and to get mace to spray in his ugly face. She kept fit, doing push-ups and sits ups every day. She learned Judo defense moves, she read about stun guns, even electric cattle prods. Just the thought of using a cattle prod on Mark was rewarding in itself. Her anger and fear of Mark had sparked her primal survival instincts. She wasn't messing around with a no-account loser like Mark.

The hell with needing a man to take care of her, that was the olden days, the strict patriarchal church propaganda teachings to manipulate and control people. Just as religious taught social norms were forced onto society by way of shame and catholic guilt controlled the population. Missy observed her co-workers and friend's marriages and figured out their guys really did not take care of them. By her observations and listening to her co-workers and friends complain all the time, she realized some guys turned out to be big babies, like another child in the family, wanting their wife-mother to take care of them.

Even at a young age Missy observed family-gathering arguments and began to figure this out. It was exactly the way her father was too. Missy decided, for now anyway, she was much better on her own. Men like her father and men like Mark had erased any trust she might have had and ingrained in her a deep lack of trust regarding men in general. In her experiences, they were just users. She could take care of herself; she had been doing that all her life anyway.

Her father beat her mother. Her father abused her repeatedly until she finally fled and ran off when she was sixteen. At first, she lived with an aunt and uncle in the next town over, but they turned out to be abusive too. And when she fought with them, the uncle called her father to come get her. She over-heard the phone call and immediately threw her things together and used baby-sitting money she had secretly hid away to get on the next bus out of town. The little money she had took her as far as St. Louis where she ended up working at McDonald's and made shared a co-worker's apartment.

Chapter Thirty

Mark was a mess. He was hurting. He did manage to drive himself home but not without getting blood all over his clothes and inside of his truck. He was crying, he hurt so badly. When he got home in the house, he immediately searched the bathroom medicine cabinet for something to put on his wounds. There was nothing for his crushed ego, he would just have to contend with that, probably with his old dependable standby, alcohol. He screamed as he poured hydrogen peroxide on his stab wounds. It burned like hell. He searched the house further and finally found some bandages and tape to wrap his forearm and his thigh. He thought he probably needed stitches in both wounds, but this would have to do--he did not trust doctors, and hospitals even less.

He vowed to get revenge when it came to Missy. His head was swimming with Missy's demise ideas. He hated she once again got the upper hand and took him by surprise. He had no idea that a weak little slut like

Missy would even think to carry a knife. She surely had taken him by surprise. He hated women at that point and wanted to kill them all. He vowed to go after his wife Ellen, as his drinking and mess-of-a-life was all her fault because she had the gall to leave him.

Mark felt the mess he was in was all Ellen's fault, and she had to pay. Of course, he had no idea that he was an egotistical, narcissistic fool, and thought everything was someone else's fault and never his own. He had no idea what a conscience was because he did not have one. Mark liked to project the cause of his problems on to others. Nothing was ever his fault; everything was always someone else's fault. His train-wreck of a life was all Ellen's fault, and he was determined to find her.

Then one day while going through the apps on his iPhone, Mark discovered something. When he and Ellen got new iPhones, they invited each other to the app called "Find Friends." Mark had forgotten all about the app, but he opened it up, and low and behold, there was Ellen's dot. Her dot showed her to be somewhere in Fenton, MO. It looked like her dot showed her to be at the new Amazon Distribution Center.

"Bingo," smiled Mark, "I think I just found Ellen. And what is she doing at an Amazon Distribution Center anyway?"

The Amazon Distribution Center was a very large complex built on the multi-acre site of the former Chrysler plant located in Fenton. Even if he pinpointed her dot as close as he could, he probably would not be able to gain access to the location to ever see her or get near her. But he was going to have to check it out. Then he had another thought. She has to be living somewhere, so he decided he would just have to keep checking the location of her dot from time to time throughout the day and night. He vowed to find her and get her back home very soon. Genius! He was thrilled.

Mark had a good day that day at work. He was in a good mood. He had a secret weapon. Ellen must have forgotten all about her connection with Mark via the Find Friends app, otherwise Mark was sure she would have deleted it. Of course, Mark was no dummy, he knew that the Find Friends app worked both ways. Ellen could tell where he was too; that is, if she thought to look at the app. No matter, he was determined to get to her first before she got to him. He planned to drive to the Amazon Distribution Center as soon as he got off work that day.

Chapter Thirty-One

Laura had plans to meet up with her son, Bob, at the Old Spaghetti Factory on Laclede's Landing on the river front for lunch. Laura got down to the Landing early to take some pictures of the Mississippi River and of the St. Louis Arch and the Arch grounds. Of course, absent minded her, forgot her good 35mm camera. She was happy to to use the camera on her iPhone and felt she got some great frame-worthy shots.

After she and Bob enjoyed a delicious lunch, they would take a leisurely walk on the cobblestone streets near the Eads Bridge which was built in mideighteen hundreds with iron smelted into steel. It was the first bridge to use iron and steel. Iron alone was not strong enough for such a wide-span bridge across the wide Mississippi River. And because train tracks were built under the roadbed of the bridge, iron would not be strong and sturdy enough, thus the invention of steel by Carnegie Steel. The Eads Bridge is still in use today, but not used as much for heavy traffic. Around 1965 the

St. Louis Arch was constructed, and the Popular Street bridge was built, to connect Interstate 64 in Illinois to Missouri.

"I love The Landing," expressed Laura, "I am so glad we choose the Old Spaghetti Factory to have lunch, seems like it's been years since we have been down here. Laura loved going to the Old Spaghetti Factory. She loved the exposed brick and wood interior, and all the dark-stained oak wood floors and trim around the doors and windows complemented the exposed brick walls of the restaurant.

After they read through the menu and ordered, Bob and Laura got down to the business of discussing Ellen's situation with Mark. Mark seemed to be the suspicious culprit in Sally Adams' death. The case needed to compile more investigated work. But it did not seem to be happening due to police work force overload. Action needed to be taken to bring Mark into justice, but sadly it was not happening even, though Ellen's life was in danger.

Laura told Bob that Missy's life was now in danger also, since her encounter with Mark. Missy was lucky to get out of that house when she did. But now she had to worry about Mark sitting in the parking lot at McDonald's watching her work at the drive-through window. She did it every day but she now was even more afraid to walk the few blocks home for fear of Mark harassing her.

"Yes, it was most fortunate that Ellen and I decided to check on her house when we did," said very intuitive

Laura. She knew her higher self and her guides gifted her with high intuitive capabilities, and she was most grateful.

"You probably helped to save Missy's life," Bob said feeling proud of his mother, "good thing you and Ellen were there when you were to rescue Missy. But then again Mom, you are a bit psychic and intuitive, aren't you?"

"Why yes, I am," smiled Laura. She was proud of her intuitive and psychic gifts.

"Your gifts certainly helped Dad solve crimes, and you have helped me. "You're a real treasure, Mom."

"Why thank you my dear, nice of you to notice," Laura replied. They both had a good laugh, then clinked wine glasses in a toast to honor each other.

"Here's to you, Mom."

"And here's to you, my son," Laura smiled as they celebrated a mutual admiration toast to one another. After they finished singing mutual praises to each other, they got back to work discussing the case concerning Ellen's estranged husband, Mark, who refused to sign divorce papers.

"What are we going to do about Mark? Ellen wants to divorce Mark, sell everything that was a result of that horrible marriage and start her life anew, free and clear of her burdensome, terrible husband Mark," declared Laura.

"Will Ellen continue living with you, Mom?" asked Bob. He thought it was nice his mother had a friend as a roommate to keep her company.

138

"Well, now that Ellen is working, I think she will be moving out soon and getting her own place. I will be sorry to see her go as she is great company. "

"I assumed you like having her with you. It's nice to have good company."

"Yes, Ellen has been a wonderful house guest, and it is nice to have her company. The house seemed awful empty since your dad's passing.

"I know, Mom," sighed Bob, "I miss Dad too."

"At times I feel as if your father, is helping me with little things; you know like solving problems or trying to find something I have lost around the house, like my keys or wallet." Laura's face lit up just thinking about her loving husband.

"I definitely feel Dad's presence, too. When I'am working on difficult crime cases, he works them with me, I know he does. And I know he is helping me on this Sally Adams' case too." Bob was feeling sentimental, he was missing his loving father.

"I feel that he is, too," agreed Laura.

"And as far as Mark is concerned," said Bob, "the department is coming very close to arresting him on suspicion of Sally Adams' death. We think we have gathered enough evidence to put him away for a very long time. So even with everything else, we are gaining some ground and getting closer to having him arrested.

Chapter Thirty-Two

Ellen's work shift was ending for the day. It is late afternoon when she walked out of the Amazon Distribution Center's main building. She was tired, it had been a long day of concentrating and trying to remember all the things she had just learned regarding her duties on her new job. She had just completed her training and was now a full-blown technical employee thrown full-time into the work force. The work was tedious, but rewarding in its own way, she knew she was getting purchased items to more customers in a speedy manner.

"Oh crap," said Ellen out loud to herself.

Jane, a co-worker, walking alongside her as they exited the building looked curiously at her, as if to ask, what's up? "What, what do you see?" asked Jane. She was curious about the look of fear on Ellen's face.

"I think my jerk of a husband, whom I have been trying to divorce, is parked right over there behind those cars." Ellen nodded her head in the direction where she saw the big red truck parked among the other vehicles in the huge multi-acre lighted parking lot.

"Oh, I see that truck parked there most days," remarked Jane, "I thought maybe the guy worked here."

"No, and please never go near that truck," begged Ellen, "that man is dangerous. Promise."

"Oh, for sure, I promise." Jane was sincere. She herself had been in an abusive relationship for many years and so happy to be free of it. Never again, she always told herself. Jane had learned her lesson. From now on she vowed to fly solo and make her own way in life without dragging a ball and chain along behind her. She had supported one abusive, drug addictive, lazy video-game crazed husband for years, and that was enough. She had experienced first-hand an abusive husband, and therefore definitely knew how horribly dangerous and oppressive an abusive relationship could be.

"I'm going to have to go back inside, as if I thought of something I forgot, and then go out another door to walk to my car," said Ellen, "I just do not want him to see me."

Ellen said good-bye to her co-worker and went back inside and walked to an adjacent building and went out that exit door. It was a longer walk, but it was worth it to not be harassed by idiot Mark. She would have to walk a way to get to her car. She saw the big red pick-up truck still parked a short distance away.

Ellen was just about ready to get her car keys out to unlock the driver's side door of her car when she felt a tap on her shoulder. She was startled and jumped.

"Hello, Ellen," sneered Mark, with an angry smile that spewed bad breath and displayed decaying teeth.

"What?" Ellen was shocked. Her worse fear of a nightmare had just reared its ugly head.

"Come with me, Ellen," Mark ordered with an angry tone to his voice, as he grabbed her by the arm. "I'm taking you home, where you belong."

"No," Ellen pulled away, "get away from me!" She felt angry and frightened.

Mark merely hung on to her arm and began leading her to his truck. Half dragging her as she tried to resist his tug on her arm. She was afraid of him and what he was capable of doing to her. She knew one good punch from him, and she could be dead. Mark pulled Ellen by the arm dragging her forward toward his truck. She lost her footing and fell. He continued to drag her by her arm. She struggled but managed to get up onto her feet again. He was jerking her, dragging her along behind him.

If only someone would see what he was doing and come to her rescue, she thought. Guess people do not want to get mixed up in domestic disputes, unlike Laura. At that moment she was very grateful for Laura's friendship and help. Mark took big steps and she stumbled trying to stand on her feet and keep up with him. She tripped over his feet and fell to the ground again. He angrily yanked her up by her long hair.

"Come on," ordered Mark, "get up."

Ellen could only hope security cameras were getting this on video and that someone watching and would be alerted. She probably would not show up for work tomorrow. For first time in years Ellen experienced the wonderful sense of freedom. Although her freedom seemed short-lived now. But she finally had the chance of knowing what independence felt like. She had a car, and a job, and a place to stay with her wonderful friend Laura. Laura was a godsend who offered to help her out of her mess with her ridiculous husband.

When they finally reached Mark's truck, he opened the driver's door and shoved her inside. She hurriedly scooted over in an attempt to reach the passenger side door to jump out. But before she had a chance, he grabbed her and pulled her back. He reached down and felt around under his seat for his gun until his fingers finally touched it. He grasped it and stuck the gun in her face with his finger on the trigger. She saw it and stopped moving and sat still.

"Try that again, and you are dead," warned Mark as he growled in an angry voice. "You're my prisoner now."

Mark drove like a maniac to their house holding the gun on her the whole time. As far as Mark was concerned, Ellen was his wife; and therefore, his property to do with has he wished. Mark drove like an idiot. *Where were the cops when you need them?*, wondered Ellen. They finally reached their street, and he whipped his truck in the driveway and slammed on the brakes. Ellen was crying and that made him even more mad. He hated to see her bawl like a big weak baby. His booze-soaked brain thought crying made her look weak, and he hated weak people. Her crying made him angry. He slapped her a good one.

"Come on, get out and get in the house," he angrily ordered.

"Let me go," she demanded. Mark only chuckled as he led her by the arm into the kitchen toward the door to the basement. In one quick movement he opened the basement door and shoved her down the basement steps. He watched and laughed as she fought to grab any part of the banister to keep from falling all the way down the steps to the concrete floor. Mark was right behind her, right at her heels. She feared he would push her. He did not push her down the steps, but when they got to the bottom, he pushed her onto a chair, it tipped over and she fell onto the floor. Ellen landed hard hitting her head. She felt suddenly nausea and dizzy.

"Come on get up," Mark demanded. "You're not hurt, so stop whining." He did not help her up. She somehow pulled herself up to get on the chair as he demanded.

Mark tied her hands behind the back of the chair and onto the chair spokes. He tied her feet together, then stuffed a dirty rag in her mouth and tied a rag across her eyes

"I'll get you, you bastard," she snorted to herself into the rag as he shoved it in. He couldn't make out what she was trying to convey. He just laughed at her. He had the upper hand now. He laughed at the sight of her sitting blindfolded, gagged and tied to a chair with her hands behind her back and her feet tied together.

He didn't care what she said or thought. He laughed as he turned to head up the basement steps and shut the basement door. She heard him lock it.

She thought she was there the rest of the day and night, it was hard to tell being blindfolded. She was frightened, hungry, tired and ached all over. Only once did he come down with a ham and cheese sandwich and let her go to the basement bathroom, while he stood at the bathroom door and listened. She wished that there was a window that opened in the bathroom, she would have crawled out, but there wasn't. The bathroom window and one other window in the basement had been replaced with thick squared block glass that you couldn't even see through, much less open up. He stood guard with gun in hand. When she was finished in the bathroom she was directed to sit back down on the chair.

"Why do you have to tie me up? You know how claustrophobic I am," she pleaded.

"No, you're not," smarted back Mark.

Mark proceeded again to tie her hands and feet to the chair and gag her, because he said he was tired of listening to her whining. And then he blindfolded her again. He did not want her to know what time of day it was, and what day it was. He wanted to mess with her mind and left her down there. He said he had to go to work and headed up the steps. When he got to the top, she heard him lock both locks on the basement door.

What the hell had just happened? She was imprisoned now and who knows for how long. After Mark left,

Ellen sat there blindfolded, gagged and tied to the chair. She sat there in shock for a few minutes trying to make sense out of what had just happened to her. She felt like crying. Then she thought of Laura. What would Laura think when she doesn't show up at home. Ellen could feel her iPhone in her pants pocket. Mark didn't take it from her. Ellen thought that he probably didn't notice it. She could not get to it with her hands tied up behind the back of the chair.

With all the stress she was under, Ellen was surprised when she had a brilliant idea suddenly pop into her head. She knew that Laura was intuitive and psychic, so she used her mind to meditate and concentrate to try to telepathically communicate with Laura. She meditated. She concentrated very hard. She wanted Laura to come find her. She had nothing better to do being tied up, gagged and blindfolded, so she concentrated on connecting mind-to-mind with Laura. She gave it her best effort as she could not see any other way of getting out of her current imprisoned predicament. If she did get herself untied, she was double locked in the basement. She felt very trapped, and Laura was her only hope. So she spent her time concentrating on Laura wanting to make a mind-to-mind connection.

Chapter Thirty-Three

It was a lovely day for Laura and Emma's walk in the park. Their walk is Emma's time, she gets to snoop wherever she wants along the path as they walk. So, it's slow going and Laura wanted to get some exercise. When they got back home, Laura changed into her biking clothes and got her bike out. Laura loved to ride her bike. It was her way of meditating, and she found that riding her bike cleared her head.

It was a good workout too for thinking, maintaining good balance, staying fit, and building strength. It was work riding in the park with all the hills, but Laura found that she loved the road-bike's drop handlebars pull on her upper arms and inner thighs especially while climbing hills. Her stomach muscles got a great work out too while climbing up the steep hill along Skinker Boulevard, which was the longest and steepest hill in the park. And there were plenty of other hills to climb in the thirteen-hundred plus acre park six-mile path around the park. Riding alone exchanging greetings with runners, walkers, and other cyclists brightened Laura's spirits. Riding on the flatter terrains she coasted a bit, and her mind began to wonder to thoughts of her friend Ellen.

She was worried about Ellen because Ellen did not come home after she got off work. Laura could sense something was terribly wrong with Ellen. She also sensed a curious urgency surrounding Ellen. Suddenly Laura realized that Ellen might be in serious trouble. Laura concentrated hard and felt a mind-to-mind connection then, as if Ellen was thinking of her too. She had the urge to call her, so she stopped and got her iPhone out and tried, but again there was no answer, and her call went to Ellen's voice mail.

Just then a vision interrupted her thoughts. It was a vision of Ellen in constraints. She was worried and frightened for her friend, and the feeling would not leave her. Laura had looped the park, and while riding on the straight-away along Lindell Boulevard, she decided to head back home. She rode as fast as she could. As soon as she got home she quickly put her bike away, hurried and changed her clothes, and took Emma for a quick walk before getting Emma in the back seat of her Prius.

Emma loved the seat belt halter that Laura put on her that was just for her. It was designed so Emma could wear the seat belt. As the seat belt fit through and latched onto the halter. Emma appeared to feel more secure wearing the seat belt halter. It held her stable and she did not have to try to keep her balance by rocking her feet side to side as she sat on the seat. Laura could tell that Emma felt more secure in the seat belt halter, too. Emma loved car rides. In fact, Emma loved her rides so much Laura discovered if Emma did not feel the ride was long enough, she would not get out of the car, but just sit in protest. Today was not going to be one of those days as Laura could tell that Emma could sense Ellen's telepathic urgency too.

"Okay Emma," Laura talked sweetly to her, "we are going to go find our friend Ellen, can you help me with that?" Emma was ready to go. Laura had the feeling that Emma knew something was wrong, and that Ellen was missing.

Laura headed over to Ellen's house. She was glad to see that the big red pickup truck, with the dual rear wheels adorned with obnoxious chrome naked lady mud flaps was nowhere to be seen. Laura parked her Prius a little way from the driveway to the house and she and Emma got out and walked toward the house. As she walked she concentrated her thoughts on Ellen. She wanted to make and keep a mind-to-mind connection. Emma seemed to be very interested in something by the solid cubed glass basement windows. She sniffed and whimpered. She began pawing at the ground below the window and scratching on the frame around the window. Laura wanted to look inside but it was impossible as those windows were the solid glass block windows. She could not see inside but she had a strong intuitive feeling that maybe Ellen was in the basement.

"Come on, Emma," directed Laura, "we need to get inside." She walked to the side kitchen door. It was locked. She walked around to the front of the house and tried the front door, it was locked. The windows she passed all seemed to be locked as she tried to lift and open each one of them. She walked further around the house and near the garage. It was there that she spotted a huge doggie door. It had a canvas sheet hanging down covering the opening. She stood in front of it studying it for a moment. It appeared Emma could easily fit and get through it, and Laura thought that if she turned sideways a bit that she would be able to maneuver and get her shoulders and hips through it. She only hoped that the other side of the doggie door was passable and not blocked in some way and that she would be able to gain access to the rest of the house. The only way to find out was to try, so she got down on all fours, feeling like a dog herself for a second. She turned around and had to laugh as she watched as Emma's had her head cocked in curiosity; as if she was trying to figure out what Laura was doing going through her doggie door. It was so comical that Laura had to laugh to herself. Emma's face as if to say, that doggie door is meant for me, not you.

Laura struggled a bit, but she managed to wiggle-waggle her way through the big doggie door. As she stuck her head through and looked around, she saw that she was in a breezeway like passage between the house and the garage. She called for Emma to follow her, and Emma was all too happy to oblige. Surprisingly enough ninety-eight-pound Emma had to get down and struggle a little bit herself, but she proudly managed and entered the room behind Laura. So now they were both inside and ready to look for Ellen. Laura only hoped that the door from the breezeway to what she figured would be the kitchen was not locked. For grins she tried the opposite door first to the garage and it was locked. So she did not feel too foolish after all coming through the doggie door when she really could have tried to jimmy and open the garage door. Once again her intuition had been in action, she figured.

Laura had her fingers crossed when she turned the doorknob and was so happy to discover that the door to the kitchen opened and was not locked. She was so grateful for that. As she entered the kitchen, she looked around, took a quick walk through the house, the bedrooms, the bathroom, and then came back into the kitchen to find Emma snoopy around and whining as she sniffed at the basement door.

"She is down there, isn't she?" stated Laura. Emma whimpered and continued to sniff at the basement door.

Laura saw the basement door had double locks, a slide lock and a dead bolt lock, and both were in the locked position. Her intuition was telling her that she was very close to finding Ellen. She only hoped and prayed that Ellen would be alive and well. Her worrying got in the way of her common sense and intuition sometimes, she had to remind herself of that. In her mind, intuitively, she knew that Ellen was okay, but emotions always took the negative point of view, which she hated. She would have to work on that and try to keep a positive attitude because she knew that thoughts create realities.

As we are all spiritual beings experiencing life on Earth as human beings and our bodies are our soul's vehicles created in order to experience our Earth's journey.

Laura prepared herself to unlock and open the basement door. She was afraid of what she might find, but she was determined to keep a positive mind-set. Emma patiently stood by her side and waited, watching and listening. Slowly Laura got the locks unlocked and slowly she opened the door. She saw that at the bottom of the steps there a dim light glowing in the otherwise silent and darkened cavern. Slowly and carefully Laura crept down the steps, Emma cautiously stepping, staying close behind. At the bottom of the stairs in the dim light she saw the horrific sight of Ellen blindfolded, gagged, and constrained by ropes. Her head lowered onto her chest. Laura saw that Ellen had been tied to a chair, her feet crossed and tied in front of her; her hands were tied to chair in back of her. It was frightening and just plain scary for Laura. She was afraid to walk up close, afraid of what she might find.

"Ellen," she whispered, her stomach tight with fear.

"Wha," Ellen managed to make a sound through her gag and ever so slightly lifted her head. She made another sound that sounded more like a moan more than a word.

"Ellen, it's me Laura," she said ever so happy to see that Ellen was alive and conscious.

"Wha," Ellen moaned again.

"Jesus, this is awful!" Laura could not believe what she was seeing. She quickly undid the gag, the blindfold, untied Ellen's hands and then her feet. It took Ellen a minute or two to even move. Carefully she began stretch a little and try to move more. Her eyes adjusting to the dimly lit basement.

"You poor thing," cried Laura, "what a monster he is."

"This has been awful," was all that Ellen could manage to whisper in that moment. Later she shared with Laura that it was a most horrific experience to be in a conscious like coma, where she could not move, speak or see, only listen. The only thing she could try to do was stay calm, breath, remind herself to stay calm, and try to relax. She just lowered her head and prayed the whole time. She had lost track of time. She had no idea if it was day or night, or even which day it was. She knew she was going to suffer posttraumatic stress after such a horrendous experience.

"Oh, thank god," whispered Ellen, slowly getting her bearings together. She had dozed off, she thought, and then hearing Laura's voice was like a gift from heaven. The experience had been traumatic for Ellen. She had been in a weird limbo like state that she never wanted to be in again. The only thing she could do was pray and meditate and concentrate her thoughts on Laura's thoughts and hope that somehow she made a mind-to-mind connection. She could only hope that Laura got her messages of needed help that she was sending to her.

"It's so wonderful to see you and Emma," smiled Ellen through tears of joy and relief.

"I believe you summoned me to this very spot, didn't you?" Laura asked Ellen with a smile.

"Yes, I did," Ellen answered with a surprise tone, "and it worked!"

"Yes, good things happen when great minds work together," Laura was happy too. She loved her intuition and psychic capabilities and had shared some incidents of such with Ellen on their dog walks. So Ellen had learned from Laura that our thoughts are very powerful.

We are all of one universal mind consciousness. Laura knew everyone had these capabilities if only they knew they existed. But she also realized that religious and elitist political and educational agendas do not want people to know just how powerful their minds and thoughts really are and that we can connect with others, even heal ourselves and others. It's done more often than we think. We can make things happen just by using our minds. Stress and our emotions can make us sick and can also heal us by us making changes in our actions and thoughts. We also have archangels waiting our request for their help, to come to our aid, we just need to ask them for help. We need to then thank them too, for all spirits, rather in the physical human form or not, like to be appreciated.

See, Laura always believed that was part of the deal volunteering to reincarnate on planet Earth, it is like this perhaps: "You go, and we'll help you when you get there, just ask us. We are at your service." People just need to think to ask their guides and archangels for assistance, even if it's just to find a parking space. They are only too happy to help.

Ellen gave Laura and big hug, while Emma pranced around a bit. She wanted a hug too. Then Ellen happily knelt down and lovingly obliged Emma.

"Come on let's get you out of here," urged Laura helping Ellen get up and making sure she had enough strength just to walk a bit and climb the steps to get out of the basement.

With Laura's aid and helping hand, Ellen made it up the stairs. She was still stiff, a little disoriented and weak but very determined to get out of that house. Ellen could not remember when she ate last. They left the house through the kitchen door. Laura looked around to make sure the coast was clear and that no big red pickup truck was coming down the street and turning into the driveway as they attempted their escape.

"The car is parked just a little way down the street," directed Laura. She hoped that Ellen would be able to walk that far. "Are you going to be okay to walk to the car?" asked Laura, "if not, you could wait here and sit down, while I get the car and come pick you up."

"I see your car," Ellen said in a weak voice, "and I think I can walk that far. I just want to get away from this place." They walked gingerly then, Laura helping Ellen. They followed Emma as she happily led the way to the car.

Laura helped Ellen get in on the passenger side and then she opened the back door and helped boost Emma up on to the seat and fastened her in. Emma always loved that boost. Laura always had to smile, she didn't know which Emma liked better, the ride or the butt boost up onto the seat. Of course, she could had gotten in by herself, a Prius doesn't sit up that high off the ground, but Laura boosted her a bit just one time and after that, Emma would put her front feet on the seat and then wait for Laura to give her a little butt boost so she could get her back feet than on the seat. Emma always expected that as part of the routine now, every time, and she never forgot, not even once.

"I can't wait to get home and get cleaned up," Ellen sighed. She felt horrible, and just plain dirty from being around the evil energy of that horrible man.

"What can I fix you to eat when we get home?" Laura was worried about Ellen. She thought Ellen looked thin and drawn and depressed. Of course, who wouldn't be after what she has been going through with that horrible man.

"Maybe I'll just start with just some toast and some sliced peaches." Ellen reverted back to a childhood memory of comfort food that her mother served her when she was ill with a bad cold or getting over the flu. Her mother always gave her toast and a little dish of canned sliced peaches.

"I hope we have some peaches," Laura said with concern. She did not remember ever seeing peached among the canned goods.

"Oh yes we do, Ellen said with delight. "I had bought some just the other day. I guess I am even more intuitive and psychic than I thought." Ellen thought she hadn't thought of toast and peaches in years. She probably bought them because of the stress surrounding Mark's behavior. Or was it a premonition of things to come. Did her intuition know that she would need very special comfort food after a horrific ordeal with her abusive husband?

"What a dreadful experience you had," Laura was sympathetic and gently patted Ellen's arm.

"Well, it certainly wasn't just a walk in the park, that's for sure. It was very scary, I had no idea what day it was, seems I have lost all track of time."

"Let's see, today is Saturday. And yesterday when you got off of work was when he snatched you off the parking lot," explained Laura.

"Saturday, oh good, I did not miss any work then. I just did not want to miss any work, being it's a new job."

"Well, I'll have Bob and his friend get your car," stated Laura, "and bring it back at the condo."

"Oh, thank you, I forgot about my car still being at work. You're a treasure, thank you so much."

As soon as they got to Laura's condo, Ellen mustered up enough energy to take a shower. The hot clean water felt so good. She just wanted to wash the whole horrible experience away and down the drain. The shower seemed to help, and she felt so much better afterward. It rejuvenated her a bit. She perked up even more after eating the toast and peaches Laura set out for her. Her energy was not long-lasting, and she wanted to make sure that she would be ready for a long day of work on Monday, so she planned to rest up until then.

"Think I'll lay down a take a nap," Ellen yawned. She was feeling tired and drained physically and emotionally. She got up and headed for her bedroom.

"I'm sure the sleep will do you good. Let me know if you need anything." Laura was glad to have her friend back home safe and sound. But she worried just what other sort of pranks and tricks did Mark have up his sleeve. Maybe Bob could help. Laura got out her phone and called her son.

Chapter Thirty-Four

"Bob," Laura was always glad to hear her son's voice. He was the love of her life, "it's your mother."

"Hi, Mom, what's up?" He was at his desk at work going through paperwork which included a list of unsolved cases, otherwise known as cold case files.

"Well son, I've got news," informed Laura. She proceeded to tell her son how she found Ellen in the basement, and that it was Ellen's husband, Mark, who tied her up and locked her in the basement of their house.

How did he find her at her work? Bob wondered. Bob worried because if Ellen's husband could find her at her new job, what was to keep him from finding Ellen at his mother's condo. He worried that his mother may be in danger.

"I don't know how he found out that she was working at the Amazon Distribution Center in Fenton. But that was where he was waiting for her with a gun. He dragged her to his truck, then drove her to their house where he proceeded to push her down the basement steps. He tied her up, blindfolded and gaged her and left her locked in the basement."

"Interesting," said Bob sitting back in his desk chair loosening his tie, he hated wearing ties. He felt like he was being choked. He scratched his dark curly head of hair that he wore a bit long, covering the tops of his ears. He liked it like that even though the captain, an ex-military man, frowned upon his non-military haircut. Bob just chalked it up to the bald captain being a little jealous of his curls. Laura always said he got his curls from his father, certainly not from her. She envied his thick hair. Laura felt hers was thin and what they used to call "dish-water blonde" in her youth. She tinted her long hair a dark blonde, for years now. Laura hated gray hair and planned to keep coloring it. While listening to Bob, Laura glanced at her reflection in the mirror above the fireplace. She needed a touch-up soon, the gray was showing, maybe tomorrow she would get to that. Right now, she wanted to help Bob solve this case.

"Bob, we have to get this guy arrested. Can't you just bring him in and off the streets for some other minor misdemeanor charge, like running a stop sign, expired tags on his license plates, just anything. He's a menace to society!"

"Wish I could," sighed Bob, "we are trying to get the legal department to take action by ordering a search warrant."

Chapter Thirty-Five

Mark's shift had ended and drinking a few beers at their usual bar after work with the guys had ended. He slowly drove home as he was feeling rather tipsy after the last beer, which he knew he should not have had in the first place. He was feeling angry when he arrived home, thinking and wishing his old lady would have dinner on the table. Then his drunken brain remembered he had his old lady tied up, blindfolded, and gagged in the basement. He had to chuckle to himself when he remembered. It was the perfect place for her. He thought he was brilliant. Well, he thought he was brilliant until he got into the house and saw that the basement door was unlocked.

"What!" He managed to mutter to himself. He knew he had locked both locks. He slowly and cautiously pulled open the basement door. It was dark down there except for the single dim lightbulb that did not provide much light. It took a minute or two for his eyes to adjust to the dimness. He slowly crept down the steps not sure what he was going to find. Once his eyes adjusted to the dim light of the basement, he noticed the tipped over chair and the ropes and gag and blindfold lying on the floor. Ellen had escaped.

"Shit," he cursed in the dreary dark empty hollow cavern of a basement. "How in the hell did she get out?" He was truly puzzled and frankly quite amazed. In his drunken stupor It was like he witnessed the mastery of a magical Harry Houdini disappearing stunt. He stooped down, which made him instantly dizzy, picked up the chair, and sat down. He had to sit down for a spell and collect his thoughts about what had taken place. The whole ordeal felt rather other-worldly, like Ellen had some secret powers, like black magic or something. His drunken brain had a wild imagination. Maybe he shouldn't be messing with her, he thought. The whole ordeal made him feel rather faint. He felt a little better after a few minutes. Finally, he figured he felt weak because he needed to fix himself something to eat. He climbed back up the steps, he would worry about Ellen later.

Chapter Thirty-Six

Ellen slept rather restlessly that night. She woke up periodically feeling constrained and found it hard to breathe. She managed to force herself to go to work Monday morning and each day thereafter. In fact, she welcomed the distraction even though she was a bit tired from lack of proper sleep. She continued to wake up at night from repeated nightmares. Each night she relived the horrid experience of being bonded, blindfolded, gaged and confined to a chair where she could not move for a long period of time. It all took its toll on Ellen. It was like being in a mental, emotional, physical torture chamber. She was shaken up and depressed by the experience, but mostly, she was angry. Anger, she came to believe was the more appropriate sentiment she felt after the horrific ordeal she faced. She wanted revenge, she just had enough!

And for some unknown reason Ellen felt Mark was not being sot after. She felt he was given a free ride. Surely the police had enough evidence. So what was the hold up? Were they waiting to see if Mark would actually kill her, then go after him and put him away for the rest of his life. Ellen refused to be harassed and dominated by Mark. This was not just a walk in the park, she had had enough. This time she was setting the trap to entrap him, at his own game. Ellen had a plan for her day off.

Since Ellen had worked through the weekend that week, she had a couple of days off during the week. So on her first day off, she drove over to their house when she knew Mark would be at work. Although she had keys, she was curious and she too discovered that she could fit through the doggie door just as Laura did and gain entrance into the house.

"Just a walk in the park," she smiled to herself as she went headfirst and wiggled a bit sideways to get her hips through the small opening. Ellen smiled as for some reason she caught herself saying that statement a lot lately. She often thought, might as well just think of life, no matter how troublesome it is as "just a walk in the park."

Once in the house, Ellen walked around quickly and looked in every room. She brought a baseball bat with her from the trunk of her car. It took all the courage she could muster, but she finally managed to make herself go down and look around in the basement. There in the soft light of the dimly lit bulb, she saw that the chair and the ropes were still strewn about on the basement floor. It was later in the day and Ellen knew Mark would be coming home very soon. She desperately wanted to surprise him.

With baseball bat in hand, she hid in the kitchen corner opposite the basement door which she left open. She was quiet. She figured out about what time he would be home after he got off of work and spent a little time with his work buddies throwing down a few beers, then he would come home rather tipsy. Perfect, she thought. He would be off balance with a fuzzy alcohol induced malfunctioning brain. Mark is going to have an accident and if he does survive the fall, the plan was to tie him up, blindfold and gag him. Just like he did her. Two can play this game. Oh yeah, she had had enough!

It wasn't long before Ellen heard loud mufflers and then saw the big red pickup truck pull in the driveway. For her own sense of added security she held onto the baseball bat tightly in front of her chest with both hands. She stood quietly waiting, holding her breath. He would be coming in and walking right past her. She would be ready with her Louisville Slugger in her hands and ready to swing it and knock one out of the ballpark. She already imagined in her mind one good whack, and he would go flying down the basement steps. Just a walk in the park.

Mark was drunk as usual when he came noisily into the house. He tripped over the rug as he came in. He was stumbling and practically bouncing off the walls, knocking things over. Ellen stood hidden from sight in the corner, she was ready for him to walk past her. It felt like it took him forever to get in front of her. Finally, when he got right up to passing the open basement door. She saw he looked at it rather strangely as if he was trying to remember if he left that door open or not. He was drinking more because of the mysterious event of Ellen's magical Harry Houdini disappearing act unnerved him to his core. He actually believed she must have gotten herself out of the ropes without help. *But how did she unlock both locks on the basement door?*, he stood and wondered.

Mark was contemplating that fact when all of a sudden, he felt a spark pain on the side of his upper back that knocked him off balance. He went flying, just as Ellen had wanted. With gut-wrenching fear and the awe and wonder of flying through the air and the uncertainty of not knowing how or where you were going to land, struck a sharp sense of fear into Mark's heart. This was not going to end well he realized, especially when Ellen's words rang loud and clear as he went airborne, "Take that asshole."

"Take that asshole," Ellen had yelled, when she swung at Mark's head but missed and hit his upper back and shoulder. He went flying. She could tell he didn't know what hit him as he lost his balance, stumbled and then went flying down the basement steps bouncing off the handrail.

It was like slow motion, Ellen thought as she watched him. She thought he would never get to the bottom. Finally, she thought, as she he landed on the floor, out cold or dead, she wasn't sure. She did not care! She thought she heard him moan. Suddenly, she got very scared. She felt feelings of dread, as if she had turned into something evil like he was, for striking back, for getting revenge. She realized in that moment that she just lowered herself to his failing standards. This was something rotten Mark would do, certainly not her. She was not proud of what she did, but she had to admit for a second, it did feel good.

Ellen felt good seeing Mark spread out on his back on the basement floor for a second, and then it freaked her out. It brought her back to her civil rational senses, just what was she doing, she was becoming like him. She hated the thought. Reality set in then, she realized she may have killed him. She became fear struck. She quickly left the house, baseball bat still in hand, as if she could not release the instrument of death from her own evil hands. She felt terrible. She wasn't a violent person. It frightened her to think that she was actually becoming like him, a brutal monster. She quickly ran to her car, threw the bat in the truck where it landed next to the softball, glove and catcher's mask and mitt. She got the idea to bat Mark a good one after she had bought the set as co-workers were starting a softball league. When she felt the bat in her hands, she felt strong and powerful, and it had given her revenge ideas, she thought she got it out of her system now. If not, she'll just have to knock one out of the ballpark during that upcoming game. A home run would be very satisfying.

On the drive back to Laura's place, Ellen collected her thoughts and her sense of being. She wasn't like him. Intuitively she knew he was still alive, but she also knew he would be very angry. She was little worried and felt she would have to act normal, as normal as she could under these horrid circumstances. She was frightened. She had a chance to turn her life around. She had a great friend in Laura. Oh, she could never tell Laura. What had she done? She just got a great job, soon she would be able to pay back money for her car Laura loaned her. . She would be able to move from Laura's condo and get her own place. All she wanted was a small condo or apartment and a sense of freedom and peace. She wanted the right to be herself, to see what she could accomplish through her own merit. She wanted to have the right to run her own life as she saw fit to suit her own needs, period.

Chapter Thirty-Seven

The concrete basement floor was hard and cold. Mark lay there stretched out. It took him a while to finally realize what had just happened. In his drunken stupor he laid there and tried to take inventory of all his aches and pains. He ached all over. As far as his fogging brain could tell, nothing felt broken. His head hurt like hell, but he realized that was the normal everyday hangover state he was usually in by this time of day.

"Damn, I must have fallen down the steps," moaned Mark laying on his back looking up at the steps. "Damn," cried Mark rubbing the bump on the back of his head--he must have hit the floor hard. His upper back really hurt. He felt like a Mack truck ran over him.

"Good thing I was drunk and therefore relaxed and limber, I might have died," Mark said to himself out loud to empty silence. He could always find justifications for his drunken stupor stunts.

Sitting up on the floor, Mark took a minute to gain his composure before trying to get up on his knees and then trying to use the support post in an attempt to pull himself up to a standing position, it wasn't happening. He was shaken to the core, for sure. The fall freaked him out. He kept trying, finally from a kneeling position and while hanging onto the post, he finally managed to pull himself up onto his feet. He leaned against the post for a few minutes to support himself and gather strength to tackle the steps.

"Now for the steps," he murmured out loud to himself.

Slowly, very slowly, he managed to limp over to the staircase. There, he took one step at a time hanging onto the banister then stopping to sit on the steps to rest. He could not make it to the top without sitting and resting for a moment before he continued his climb. He thought someone would have thought he was attempting to climb Mount Everest, seeing the way he struggled. He was a sight to behold the way he struggled to breathe as if the high mountain air was too thin to deliver enough oxygen to his foggy alcohol-soaked brain. It took him a while, but he finally made it to the top into the kitchen. Slowly he managed to make it through the kitchen to the bathroom where he took further inventory of himself and his possible injuries. He feared internal injuries. His head, ribs and back hurt the most.

Mark was just in poor health overall. He had not been feeling too good of late. It frightened him to see his face in the mirror. He avoided looking, only looking when he had to, to shave, and then he tried to keep his eyes closed. Was it his imagination or did the whites of his eyes seem to look a little less white and more yellow. Jaundice! The thought scared him. That meant he had liver problems. He was pissed. Mad that he was probably very ill and mad that his Harry Houdini of a wife-witch managed to escape his grasp. He could not stand for this. He had to find her and teach her a lesson, and he would as soon as he felt a little better, maybe in a day or two; but for now, he needed to lay down, so he was headed for the closest thing, the couch. He needed to lay down.

Chapter Thirty-Eight

Ellen was becoming more fearful, so Laura and Emma continued to drive Ellen to and from work each day. Otherwise, Ellen wanted to stay home and in doors at Laura's condo and not go to work, for fear of Mark harassing her there and kidnapping her again, or worse. She didn't tell Laura that she took a bat to Mark. She also thought since he was drunk and limber that the fall to the basement did not harm him all that much. And she imagined Mark just thought he tripped, lost his balance, and fell down the steps. But in any case, she figured by now since she had escaped her basement imprisonment that Mark was out for blood. She feared for her life. So each day she proceeded with caution.

"What can I do?" asked Ellen. She and Laura were sitting at the breakfast bar having coffee and discussing her situation with Mark. "I'll talk to Bob today," confirmed Laura, "hopefully he can get a quick restraining order against Mark to try to keep him away from you until we get him arrested and out of the way."

"I just can't understand the holdup," complained Ellen. She wondered what was taking so long to get this horrible person off the streets.

"The detectives' workloads are overwhelmed with cases. My son said they need more detectives on the force to help him out."

"I am so afraid, I do not want to end up in that basement again," confessed Ellen, "I am just so grateful that you taught me to be more intuitive and to use my mind, but I know I don't want to have my life depend on that again; once was enough."

"Oh, for sure, I received your mental messages, we were mind-to-mind connected, weren't we" Laura was proud of Ellen for thinking of it and told her so. "You did a great intuitive job."

"I was never so happy to see you." Ellen was so grateful.

"Yes, that was good thinking on your part. I see you have learned a bit and picked up a few things hanging around with me."

"I'm so glad I thought of it. Besides, It was all I had left to use, being locked up, gagged, blindfolded and bound to a chair in pitch darkness. It was like my mind was solely connected to the universe."

"Well, Emma was a big help," stated Laura, "she went to the square-block basement window right away and pawed at the side of it to let me know you were down there."

"You both are my heroes who have helped me so much."

"And we will continue helping and looking out after you, because Emma and I will continue to drive you to and from work each day until Mark gets arrested."

"You will?"

"Of course."

"I can never repay you for all that you have done for me," Ellen said with tears in her eyes.

"Hey, it's just a walk in the park, as you say." Laura replied with a smile. "It's my pleasure, besides, you are allowing me to play detective, and that makes me happy and my son happy. He and I are getting together for lunch today to talk more about your case."

Ellen felt so much better after learning that Laura and Emma would continue to drive her to and from work each day. For her safety they would continue dropping her off and picking her up right at the door until Mark was arrested.

Laura noticed for several days when she and Emma went to get Ellen from work, that the big red pickup was parked in the parking lot a distance away from the door. Emma would growl when she saw the big red pickup truck. She had picked up Mark's scent from the house. She knew there was a bad man sitting inside that truck. Laura knew he was sitting in the truck spying and waiting for his chance to get another crack at kidnapping Ellen, or worse. Ellen and Laura both thought he was reaching the end of his patience, and that if he got hold of Ellen again, it could be fatal for her.

It worked perfectly, Laura dropped Ellen off at the building's door and picked her up right there too. And

Emma was always along for protection, and for the ride, since Emma loved to ride in the car. As soon as Laura would pick up her keys from the hallway table, Emma was right there with her leash in her mouth, wagging her butt, as she had just a stump of a tail, so the whole backend wiggled from side to side. And Laura got use to their twice a day rides too, sometimes after dropping Ellen off at work, Laura and Emma would walk in Fenton Park or along the Meramec River Trail before they headed back home.

On this particular day, after they walked the Meramec River Trail, Laura had planned to meet Bob at a restaurant on Lucid in the Central West End and eat outside on the sidewalk patio. Emma could go along because being outside, she was permitted to lay at their feet. When they arrived, Laura spotted Bob already seated at a patio table. He spied them too when Laura and Emma came walking around the corner from the parking lot.

"Hi, Bob," greeted Laura, "well this is very nice and such a pleasant setting on a beautiful day," She gave her son a quick hug when she and Emma got to the table.

"Hi, Mom," Bob got up to hug her, "I ordered an iced tea for you with lemon, like I know you like it." Bob pulled out a chair for his mother to sit next to him after he gave a quick hello pat on the head and scratch behind the ears to Emma. Emma immediately knew her place under the table, well mostly under the table. She was bigger than the table and their feet were in the way. But she managed. This was a big deal for Emma to get to go to lunch with the grown-ups. She knew to behave so Laura would keep taking her along.

Laura had Emma lay on the side by the fencing and bushes out of the way from the waitress' feet. Emma was happy, she loved being with people. She knew to behave when other owners with dogs walked by, even though she felt temped, she knew better. It seemed the dogs behaved as if they knew if they acted up, they would not be invited back again. Emma lay quietly while Bob and Laura ate their salads and sandwiches and talked detective work stuff.

"Our crazy caseload is such that, it is a wonder I got a lunch break in at all today," explained Bob.

"I wish I could help," Laura was a detective at heart. She told Bob how she and Emma found Ellen blindfolded, gagged and bound to a chair in her basement. And that she and Emma were now driving Ellen to and from work each day. Laura also told Bob they see Mark's truck parked in the parking lot of Ellen's work most days. They both realized Mark was there every day, stalking her as he sat in his truck hoping to spot and nab her when the chance arose.

"Yes, we have to get this guy. I will try to move his case closer to the top of the stack, all the way to the top, if I can swing it."

Bob had to get back to work so they bid their farewells. But it was such a lovely day Laura and Emma walked a bit around the Central West End, they walked over to Laclede Avenue across from Barnes Jewish Hospital and sat outside at Panera's visiting with the other dog owners who were taking advantage of the warm sunshine on a beautiful day.

"Come on, Emma," Laura looked at the time, "we better get going it's about time to pick up Ellen." Emma ears perked up, she was ready to get back in the car again and go for a ride.

Chapter Thirty-Nine

Mark was still hurting from his tumble down the basement steps. He thought it was a good thing he was drunk, it made him more limber. Otherwise, he would have been hurt a lot worse. He still had not figured out what he had tripped on, that sent him flying down the steps. He only knew he would have to be more careful. He found his pain only fired up his anger toward Ellen. He was determined to capture Ellen, one way or another. He was angered that Ellen escaped her basement prison. He was going to have to teach her a lesson, and if someone was helping Ellen, they would need to be taught a lesson also.

After his hangover headache finally cleared up a bit and his thinking cleared, Mark remembered he found Ellen's location via the Find Friends app. He had followed her dot and that was how he discovered she worked at the newly opened Amazon Distribution Center in Fenton. He got his iPhone out and checked it. Yes, she was at work there now. His only problem was with all the alcohol abuse Mark's memory was not so good, which was much to Ellen's benefit, as Mark kept forgetting about having the Find Friends connection with Ellen on his phone. Evidently Ellen had forgotten about her Find Friends app also, because she never thought to remove Mark from the app.

Mark's headaches were getting worse. He thought perhaps he needed glasses, or maybe the problem was his sinuses. He knew that booze abuse was the main cause of his headaches. Mark was beginning to drink beer or a swig of liquor before he started work in the mornings. Ever since Sally met Mark in his truck at lunch times, he kept a bottle of Jim Beam in the truck under the seat right next to his loaded Gluck nine-millimeter handgun. Another morning, another means to a paycheck, he told himself and he took a big slug from the bottle beneath the seat before he walked over to the work site. It calmed his nerves and dulled his aching head.

Chapter Forty

"Hey there," Laura said when Ellen slide into the passenger seat, turned around and patted a happy-to-see-her, wiggling butt, Emma on the head.

"Hi, thank you so much for picking me up all these days. I'll owe you forever."

"Oh, it's just a walk in the park, as the saying goes. I am only too happy to help, and Emma loves her twice-day car rides." Laura was about to pull out of the Amazon Distribution Center when they saw the big red pickup truck entering the parking area from another near-by entrance.

"I hate the thought of the day when he is coming in the same way as we are leaving," worried Ellen.

"Well, he doesn't know me," stated Laura, "so hopefully he won't pay any attention to me or my passenger in the car with me."

"If we ever see him tailing us, then we are in big trouble," Ellen stated with a worried tone to her voice.

"Well, I think then we are in big trouble," warned

Laura, "because the big red pickup truck just made a U-turn in the parking lot, and he is coming up right behind us. There are two cars behind me keeping him off my tail, thank god they are there."

"Oh crap," said Ellen, "wish we could just call the cops on him."

"Well, right now he is not doing anything wrong, so I guess we can't," stated Laura, "sorry to say."

"Well, what happens if we can't shake him," Ellen said with a worried tone to her voice as she turned around to look out the back window, after moving around to try to see his reflection in her side mirror. "Jeez, he's about two cars behind us still."

"Well, okay then, let's take a ride west on Highway 44 then, instead of turning to go back towards the city, to Clayton," suggested Laura and she turned right onto the highway heading west. She watched in her rearview mirror; Ellen leaned forward to see the reflection in the passenger side mirror.

"Crap," sighed Ellen, "he is behind us."

"Think I'll go north on 141" said Laura, "I can make more turns onto streets and roads to see if he follows. After turning onto 141 and driving a bit, Laura got another idea.

"Think I'll get off shortly and go to Costco."

"Good idea," agreed Ellen, "let's see if he follows us there."

Laura drove like a woman with determination on her way to Costco. The parking lot was huge. She decided to get gas first before going into the store and pulled up to the pumps. As she pumped the gas she looked around in every direction for the big red pickup. Nothing.

"I don't see him."

"I think he is around here somewhere, hiding. I can feel it," admitted Ellen, "Although I don't know how you can hide a big red vehicle like that too easily. I feel his presence and it's creeping me out."

"I agree," confessed Laura, her intuition was telling her the same thing. Mark was around there somewhere.

"Well, since we are here, we might as well go in and get a few things,"

"Sounds good to me." Ellen felt she was in disguise. She was used to wearing dark glasses, with her hair tucked into a baseball cap pulled down close to her eyes. She's pulled on a big shirt she carried with her. Anything to disguise her appearance.

They thought if indeed Mark was parked somewhere nearby hidden in the parking lot eventually, he would get tired of waiting and or get thirsty for a beer and just leave. The ladies took their time, looked around and shopped in the store for at least forty-five minutes.

Chapter Forty-One

"Oh shit," sighed Mark talking to himself, "maybe that wasn't Ellen in that car after all." Mark was driving himself crazy. More than once he followed cars into parking lots of Walgreens, and CVS's and service stations thinking he was following Ellen. It was even becoming evident to Mark that the booze was taking its toll. He felt like hell. He knew the construction foreman and guys on the crew took pity on him. But he could tell their patience was running thin and they would not cover for him forever. Just how much longer were they going to follow after him, check his work and then, if necessary, redo his work, which was clearly becoming the norm to the other workers. He was more of a hinderance than a help, even Mark in his constant hangover state was beginning to realize that. Mark drove past the McDonald's where Sally had worked, and looked for Missy.

Missy was well aware of Mark's spying shenanigans. She was still paying attention to her whereabouts regarding Mark. If Missy saw him at the window where the orders were placed, she knew he would be coming to her pay window next. Workers knew the routine and quickly switched positions with her right before Mark drove up to pay so she would not have to deal with him.

Mark was disgusted that Missy was avoiding him when he came to McDonald's. In his self-pity, he mistakenly ordered twice as much food as he normally does. But when he got home and planted himself on the couch in front of the television set, he found that he easily managed to eat the burgers and fries and whatever else he ordered in his drunken stupor. With his belly full of beer and junk food, he quickly fell asleep and slept the rest of night on the couch with the lights and television still on.

Chapter Forty-Two

"Let me help you carry that," offered Ellen, as she took the big bundle of toilet paper from Laura and carried it inside the condo. The ladies had to laugh in agreement that they loved shopping in big bulk box stores. But, when it came to unloading the car that was another story, and getting big heavy boxes and containers into the house was a workout. Funny, they thought about buying fewer items, only when they got home and had to empty the car and carry things in, Finally, the big bundles of toilet paper, paper towels, big container of dog food, roasted rotisserie chicken, the fresh vegetables and fruit, frozen desserts finally were all were successfully carried inside.

"I could sit and rest now, but Bob is coming over for dinner this evening when he gets off work, but that won't be until late."

"I think Emma has other ideas about you resting," Ellen said looking at Emma sitting at the door holding her leash in her mouth and wagging her butt.

"Okay Emma, we're coming," Laura said with a smile as she got up from the couch.

Ellen slipped on her walking shoes and latched Emma's leash to her collar. The ladies got ready for their walk in the park, while Emma waited at the door happily wiggling her stump tailed butt with impatient enthusiasm.

It was a wonderful time of the day for a walk in the park. The threesome happily walked across the street into the park as the late afternoon sun casted shadows and created a cool breeze. The air was especially fresh and delightful when they reached Art Hill. They heard a classic string quartet with acoustic accompaniment in concert. It was a wonderful musical gathering, complete with food and beverage vendors set up along the drive, in front of the Art Museum. The ladies got a couple of corn dogs for themselves and to share with Emma and two lemonades and one bottle of water for Emma's portable water dish.

They had walked a bit then spied an available seat. They sat for a few minutes on one of the stone benches positioned throughout the area. They thoroughly enjoyed listening to the string quartet as they all enjoyed their treats. After a while they continued on with their walk and headed towards the zoo area and the 1902 World Fair Pavilion. It was dusk now as they walked along chitchatting about this and that and listened to the birds singing their last songs of the day. The sun was setting in the west, as the full moon rose in the east casting a brilliant glow that would be perfect to light their way for their walk back home on the path through the thick pine and oak trees. They were enjoying themselves and the beautiful evening. Unfortunately, their high moments carried a challenging low to them. They had no idea what was lurking around the corner and hiding in the shadows.

"What was that?" Laura was startled. "That sounded like a gun shot."

"Yeah, a gun shot," cried Ellen. "I think I heard the bullet whiz past my head."

"Holy shit," cried Laura, "another shot."

This time Laura thought that she had heard the bullet whiz past her head. The threesome ducked behind a huge oak tree. They heard the sound of heavy footsteps snapping fallen twigs and crunching dry leaves. The ladies stood frozen with fright. Emma sensed their concerns and knew to keep still, too. She sat at their side and the ladies could tell Emma was listening, too. She heard the footsteps and the commotion in the brush near them. Another shot was heard.

"Holy shit," cried Ellen, "Jesus, look, it landed right here in the trunk of this tree."

"We need to get out of here," whispered Laura in an urgent tone.

The ladies felt like sitting ducks. They were terrified. They knew it was Mark. Who else would be taking pot shots at them?

"How in the hell can he see clearly enough to even fire a gun?" asked Ellen. Without even having to question it, both ladies just knew it was Mark. It seemed that they were never going to escape the wrath of that maniac. They kept quiet and stayed still hoping he was leaving the area as the footsteps grew more faint. They peeped out from behind the giant oak tree and did not see or hear anything. But they still felt his presence lurking near them.

They then heard the start-up roar of a loud muffler, and smelled the fumes that permeated the area as the diesel engine turned over, headlights turned on as the truck slowly pulled away from the curve. The truck slowly headed up the street away from them, so slow they knew that he was still looking for them. Ellen was not surprised when she noticed that crazy Mark had a spotlight mounted near his driver-side mirror. They could see he was aiming the spotlight into the wooded area of the park. He was searching for them. They stayed still not daring to move, until he gave up and slowly drove on towards the park exit.

"I think he is giving up, for now anyway."

"That was scary," admitted Laura walking cautiously and looking all around.

"This has to stop because he is putting, not only me, but you and Emma in danger, , and I won't have it," Ellen said angrily

"He needs to be arrested." Laura knew it was wishful thinking.

Chapter Forty-Three

"Laura, I think I have a plan," said Ellen. But little did Ellen realize that Mark also had a plan. Ellen was still connected to his Find Friends App. Ellen never thought to make him unavailable so he could not check on her whereabouts. In fact, Ellen forgot all about it, but Mark did not. He had forgotten too, until recently and that was how he found out where Ellen was working or when they were in the park.

Mark was very amused that Ellen never thought to disengage him from her Find Friends app. He could find her approximate location anytime, and check on where she was at any given moment. Mark decided he was no longer going to wait for her to leave her work at the Amazon Distribution Center. No, he would follow her dot to where she was now staying. Mark assumed Ellen was staying with that woman who picked her up from work, who walked with her dog and Ellen in the park. And it was probably the same woman who was riding bikes with Ellen that day in the park when he grabbed Ellen and threw her and her bike in the truck. He was going to stalk her at her home where she and Ellen were living.

Mark's anger, as if accumulating compounded interest, was ready to hit a new high. Mark's mental state was getting worse, now he not only wanted to kill Ellen, he wanted to kill that woman helping her. He decided to leave them alone and let them walk back home or wherever their car was parked. From now on he was going to remember to just watch her Find Friends app dot and then entrap her in her friends' home. There was more than one way to make Ellen's life miserable. She needed to be punished for leaving him.

Chapter Forty-Four

Ellen, Laura and Emma were sitting on their patio. They just got back from picking up Ellen from work and enjoying beef tacos on the patio, with peach salsa, corn chips and iced tea. They were again going over the events on their walk in the park the evening before.

"I wonder, how did Mark know you are working at the Amazon Distribution Center in Fenton?" Laura was curious.

"You know I wondered that too. Did he follow me?"

"That would certainly take a lot of time."

"I just thought of something." Ellen's eyes opened wide with discovery.

"What?" Laura was staring at Ellen.

"My iPhone gave me away," revealed Ellen, "what else could it be?"

"Why, whatever do you mean?" Laura was puzzled.

"I have the Find Friends app. Mark is a friend on the app. I can always know where he is, and he the same with me."

"Oh crap," agreed Laura, "that does work both ways, doesn't it?"

"So, lets pull it up and see where Mark is." Ellen had to search for the app as she did not have it readily available on her iPhone home screen. She had forgotten about the app and never thought to look at it.

"It's a spy app isn't it," suggested Laura.

"Yes, it is, and the whole idea of the app was Mark's."

"Figures," stated Laura, "if he wanted to keep an eye on your whereabouts."

"Crap, no wonder he knew where to find me at work and when we were riding bikes, or walking in the park, or eating at the Boathouse. He knew our every move. It's a wonder he has not come by here when we are at home."

Just then all three of them, Laura, Ellen and Emma, were startled and jumped as they heard a loud knock at the front door.

"Crap, that scared me." Ellen jumped and her heart was racing in her chest.

"Damn, who's at the door?" exclaimed Laura, she was shaken.

"Were you expecting Bob, or anyone else?"

"No, not this evening. Holy shit. I wonder who it is."

There was no way to ignore what was becoming a persistent knock at the front door. Emma was becoming slightly disturbed and growled softly standing and staring at the door handle as if to dare the potential intruder to open the door. Well, they knew it wasn't Bob at the door because Emma told them it was not.

And Bob never ever knocked that hard. This person knocking seemed to be angry and pounding with his fist.

"Oh crap, its Mark," revealed Ellen as she had re-opened the Find Friends App and saw where Mark's dot was located - right next to hers.

"What, why?" asked Laura.

"Look see where his dot is." Ellen anxiously held her phone in front of Laura. Laura's eyes grew big.

"We need to call the cops," Laura said.

"I don't have a restraining order," stated Ellen.

"That would have helped," declared Laura with a sigh, "to get the police here sooner."

"He said he would kill me if I ever got a restraining order against him." Ellen was scared. The knocking was not letting up.

"Think I'll call Bob," Laura said as she reached for her phone. The knocking was getting louder. Laura could not figure out why the neighbors were not complaining.

"Ellen, I know you are in there," Mark hollered through the door.

"Don't say anything," commanded Laura, "that dot is not that specifically pinpointed so how does he know he has the correct condo."

"You're right, he is fishing," agreed Ellen smiling slightly meeting Laura's glance.

"Bob said he'll try to stop by as soon as he can," said Laura, "he's downtown at the scene of a shooting right now,"

"Well, I told him there just may be another shooting

over here before long, so hurry up," Laura was getting very concerned. They knew Mark had a gun because he poked it in Ellen's face when he kidnapped from her work's parking lot and shot at them while they walked in the park the evening prior. The bullets had landed in the tree next to their heads. Talk about a near death experience, thought Laura.

The ladies kept the lights off and spoke in whispers. Emma seemed to get the message too as she appeared to walk more softly so her nails wouldn't clink on the hardwood floors. Which also reminded Laura that she needed to get Emma groomed and her nails trimmed one of these days soon. She added that to her mental list of things to do.

"The patio door!" Ellen spoke a little louder than a whisper this time. They had forgotten to close and lock the patio door when they came inside.

"He's stopped knocking," Laura realized, then, "oh oh, I bet he has run around to the back."

"I'll get it," Ellen quickly headed over to close and lock the patio door. She was right up on it when the screen suddenly opened, and Mark grabbed her and yanked her out onto the patio. She screamed. She fought with all her might against big burly angry Mark. Emma tried to come to her rescue and bit Mark's leg. He yelled then kicked her and Emma let out a yelp as she rolled a complete roll before getting back up onto her feet. Mark had somehow managed to hang onto Ellen as he kicked and pushed Emma back inside and quickly slammed the patio door shut behind her. Mark had a choke hold on Ellen and was now dragging her across the patio and around the building to the front, where his truck was parked.

"Emma come," cried Laura she had taken a dive behind the couch thinking she saw a gun in Mark's hand. She was back on her feet now.

Emma ran over to Laura and nuzzled her head into Laura thigh as she stood there. Laura looked Emma over and made sure Emma was not hurt, and she did not appear to be. But Laura was furious, no one kicks my dog, she thought to herself.

Just then Emma must have heard Ellen screaming. She ran and began pawing at the front door, and Emma knows not to do that, but this was an emergency, so she figured it was okay to do so. She had to get Laura's attention to let her know that she needed out. She wanted to get her teeth into that nasty mean man's leg again.

Laura heard Emma and came running and quickly unlocked and opened the front door just as she heard Ellen screaming. Emma leaped out of the front door, jumped over the low banister, skimmed the bushes and landed on the lawn. She landed just a few yards from where Mark was dragging Ellen by her hair toward his truck. Ellen was succeeding in slowing him up by her twisting, kicking and screaming. Laura watched in horror from the opened front door. Her phone at her ear with Bob on the line who said that he was on his way--just a mile away he reported.

"Ah shit?" Mark cried out when Emma grabbed his

ankle by her teeth and jerked and yanked at it. She meant business! The fear and pain was bad enough that Mark loosened his grip on Ellen and she twisted free from him. By then Emma had Mark on the ground yanking his ankle around viciously. Mark was hollering. There was blood.

"Get'm Emma," Ellen egged Emma on, "get'm Emma."

It was a crazy scene of chaotic proportions. Laura heard the siren and saw the flashing lights as Bob's patrol car sped in her direction. He pulled up and parked along Skinker Blvd and rushed over to where Emma was standing guard over Mark. Mark could not make a move without Emma nipping at his ankles. Laura rushed over and held Ellen in her arms, as she was sitting on the grass, crying.

"Mom," Bob cried as he ran over to where the ladies were and where Emma was standing guard over Mark. Bob petted and praised Emma for the good job she did taking down and guarding the perpetrator for him. Emma continued to keep Mark down on the ground. Mark was moving around trying to get to his gun, it fell out of his pocket as he struggled; he tried desperately to reach for it. But Emma kept yanking him away every time his hand came even close to touching the gun. Emma being a ninety-eight-pound Rottweiler was doing a pretty good job of it too. Just then Bob saw the gun and swiftly kicked it away out of Mark's reach. Bob picked up the gun and held it in his hands pointing it at Mark.

"Get up," Bob demanded. He wasn't messing around. One false move and Mark would have ended up with a bullet wound in his leg to go along with the dog bites.

"Call the dog off," begged Mark.

"Sure," answered Bob, planning on taking his sweet time.

"Hurry," cried Mark, "Ouch!" He cried as Emma nipped his ankle.

"Nah, I talk slow, and Emma has a mind of her own," Bob said showing a little anger. He was being extra slow leaving fearful Mark in agony and he told Mark as much, too.

"That's for firing those shots at my mother, Ellen, and at Emma as they were just taking a walk in the park," stated Bob.

Bob let Emma give Mark a few more painful yanks then he nicely asked Emma to stop, and Emma listened and moved away and sat down next to Bob. But she kept an eye on evil Mark. Any false moves and she was going to go after him again, with pleasure.

"Okay, Emma," Bob said softly, "good girl, what a good girl you are. I should have you come to work with me. We'd get those crooks, wouldn't we, Emma?" and Emma leaned into Mark's leg for a second in admiration.

"You are under arrest for the murder of Sally Adams," Bob informed Mark. "Put your hands behind your back," Bob ordered as he prepared to handcuff Mark.

"What? I did no such thing," Mark was pleading his innocence to deaf ears.

"Oh, I think we have enough evidence to prove otherwise. Turn around," ordered Bob.

Mark was likely to spend a very long time in prison for his crimes. Ellen and Laura were pleased at the possibility of Mark being locked up and out of the way for many years.

Just before Bob could get the handcuffs on him, Mark sprang up, and quickly twisted around, and wearing steel toed work boots, landed a painful kick to Bob's groan. Bob screamed with pain and fell to the ground, doubled over. Laura and Ellen ran to him as Mark took off running, shoving Emma out of the way. Emma quickly recovered and chased after Mark as he ran to his truck. Mark raced with all his might, breathlessly he made it to the passenger side of the truck. He quickly opened the door and jumped in and slammed it quickly behind him. Just narrowly missing out on the opportunity of feeling Emma's teeth nipping at the seat of his pants. Mark quickly slid over behind the steering wheel, started the truck and peeled out in front of oncoming traffic. He nearly caused an accident as two cars had to slam on their brakes to keep from colliding with his truck.

Mark thought his best bet was to get out of town, and he drove like a maniac through red lights, narrowing avoiding accidents as he raced over to McCausland Avenue to jump on the highway. He headed West on Highway 64. He drove like a maniac switching lanes and cutting people off. He nearly sideswiped three cars in the process. Bob, still in pain lay on the ground, but managed to get his phone out and alert the police., They were in hot pursuit, but keeping a safe distance and not get innocent drivers in harm's way.

Meanwhile, Bob sat on the grass in front of Laura's condo recovering and collecting himself. He had only been too thrilled that he had managed to alert the police with the description of Mark's truck and his license plate number. Bob wanted to get Mark very badly for threatening his mother, her friend, Emma, and for kicking him. He was still in pain. He wished he was out there chasing Mark himself but was only too glad that the city police notified the state highway patrol and they were now in hot pursuit of Mark as well.

The ladies, Emma and Bob retreated back inside Laura's condo. Bob listened to police updates on his phone regarding Mark and the ongoing police pursuit. Word was that Channel 2 Fox News helicopter sky cam was hovering overhead of the car chase. So Laura turned on the television. It was OJ Simpson's Bronco pursuit all over again, only the big red pickup had the pedal to the metal. The truck, built for power, rather than speed, labored along, dual wheels singing and naked lady mud flaps, flapping in the wake of the dual wheels. Black diesel fume exhaust spewed into the air. The cops were not holding back now. They were out to get this guy. In their rearview mirror motorist heading west saw the emergency lights coming up fast behind them and pulled over. Mark had his truck gas pedal to the metal. He had it floored. The truck just didn't have speed potential, there was too much drag with the big thick treaded tires and the dual rear wheels, definitely not built for speed. Mark had it pushed to the limits as he watched the cops coming up closer and closer behind him.

Mark had that diesel engine humming. He had it floored and was surprised he was pushing over a hundred-miles-per hour. He never had it up to that speed before. He was rather proud of his old truck. He laughed and in his booze-soaked brain actually thought that he was going to out run them. He kept watching his side mirrors looking to see how close the cops were getting. He grew nervous and was shaking as he kept turning around, taking his eyes off the road, to look behind to see how close the cops were getting.

Big mistake, turning and looking around, as he took his eyes off the road just as a dangerous sharp curve was coming up just ahead and it was coming up fast. He was going much too fast for the sharp curve. The curve was not banked enough, and he knew it, but it was too late to slow down and so the centrifugal force sent him and his big red truck flying against the guardrail on the side of the road. That big of truck at such a high speed merely crashed through, but mostly flew over the top of the guardrail. It was too late, when he saw the steep drop off into the large ravine below. He screamed as the truck took a nosedive into the big deep ditch. Call it karma or not, but unlike the time he nosedived Sally's car into a ditch to pose an accident, this time, the ditch was much deeper and he knew it was endgames for him. His blacked out as the truck flipped end-over-end several times down the embankment then crashed into several big boulders and brush and burst into flames.

As the police drew near the curve, they spotted a huge ball of black smoke and flames rise up from his crash site. They called the fire department and pulled over and all they could do was watch and wait for the fire trucks to arrive. The blaze was too hot to get near. The fire engines pulled up to the scene in minutes and doused the truck fire and extinguished the surrounding brush fire. Mark was pronounced dead at the scene, and Ellen became a widow.

Chapter Forty-Five

Ellen, Bob, Laura, and Emma sat and watched the police chase on television. They saw the tragic fiery crash and witnessed the demise of Mark. According to on-the-spot news reporting, Mark was pronounced dead at the scene. No tears were shed at Laura's place, that's for sure. Only sadness and a welcomed sense of relief was felt by all.

"Hopefully, troubled Mark will find peace now," was the only kind thing that came to Ellen's mind to say. Ellen could not help but sigh with relief, finally, a sense of peace had come over her, something she had not felt for years. It was as if a huge weight had been lifted from her shoulders. She was thankful that she had survived the crazy man's torment. She wondered just how many other women had to go through similar circumstances before they found freedom.

To help other women, Ellen vowed to study psychology and criminal law so she could create a women's self-help group for women suffering from relationship and marital abuse. And she planned to write a book regarding her experiences in order to help other women learn to watch for certain signs of ongoing worsening aggression coming on and to know where and how to seek help.

"I swear, I do not know how to act," sighed Ellen, "without the threat of Mark's violent behavior looming above my head on a daily basis like a dark angry cloud. I feel as if I can breathe again."

"I am so happy for your newfound freedom," Laura expressed.

"Me too!" Ellen agreed. She was so ready to begin life anew.

"So, a fresh start for you now, and there will be a new good man to come along for you I am sure."

"Nah, I think I am getting a dog. A Rottweiler like sweet Emma." She knelt down and hugged Emma with tears in her eyes. "Thank you, Emma for coming to my rescue, you're the best ever.," Emma leaned into her.

Chapter Forty-Six

Weeks passed and Ellen's life was opening up for her now, for the first time in years she felt the sense of freedom to do as she chose, she was having fun now. She loved her job at Amazon, and they loved her. A promotion was offered, and she was on the way to more training and becoming a manager soon. She was thrilled. Her confidence was soaring. She was making good money. She was happy and proud to be able to pay back the money Laura loaned her for the down payment on her car.

Laura went apartment and condo shopping with Ellen. They had fun looking at all the various locations and apartments and condo designs. And then Laura found out that a small condo in Laura's condominium complex had just come on the market for sale. It was right around the corner from Laura's. They loved the idea of being close neighbors. So, Ellen bought the condo with the money she got form Mark's small life insurance policy and from the sale of the house that she and Mark had owned. Ellen had a blast ordering new furnishings from Amazon. She loved owning her own place and decorating it to suit her own taste. The condo was perfect for her.

She needed to experience independent thinking and planning and making her own decisions. It was wonderful to be free. She loved that her condo had a lot of light from big windows in the front and large patio doors to her roomy patio in the back. It seems each day another house decorating purchase was delivered. It was easy to buy rather cheap furniture and have it delivered. She even liked assembling the pieces herself. She got a mattress delivered in a box, of all things. She slid the box up the steps, then just opened it and rolled out the mattress onto the bed frame, that she put together herself, and let the mattress puff up. She got rid of all the old furniture that was in the house.

She wanted no reminders of that life there with him. She enjoyed ordering items online at Amazon and smiled as she used her employee discount. When the items arrived, she put the sofa and two recliner pieces together herself. She loved the design of her condo. It was an open floor plan with two bedrooms and two bathrooms. Ellen loved the wide plank hardwood floors throughout the condo. She bought four stools for her snack bar open kitchen to the living room floor plan, along with a small dining set. She loved having a fireplace. There was only one thing missing.

When Ellen got her new place all spruced up, she had Laura and Emma over for morning coffee after their walk around Forest Park. It was a lovely day and so after showing Laura all her new purchases and decorating skills, they sat on the patio and sipped coffee and ate pastry.

"Thanks for helping me," sighed Laura, "you have been a wonderful friend."

"I am only too happy to help, "just a walk in the park, as the saying goes." Then she laughed. Laura got used to using Ellen's saying, for it was true she felt.

"Yes, life was just in the park, as long as you are not shot at," added Ellen rolling her eyes. They both had to laugh.

"I just have one more favor to ask of you," smiled Ellen.

"Anything," smiled Laura.

"Come with me to find a dog. I want to get a dog."

Chapter Forty-Seven

It was a lovely spring day and as promised, Laura accompanied Ellen, on her day off from work to the Humane Society to help her pick out a dog. Laura was so excited she couldn't wait for Ellen to meet and pick out a dog that she connected with, just like she did with Emma. Ellen loved Emma so much that she wanted to get a dog for herself too.

They looked at several Humane Society locations, nothing clicked. Ellen felt she wanted to make a connection, like Laura did with Emma.

"How about we have lunch at the Boathouse in the Park," suggested Ellen, they were getting hungry, and they both loved the Boathouse.

"Sounds like a plan," smiled Laura.

"We can have a nice lunch," suggested Ellen as she parked her Prius in the Boathouse parking area, "and then we can go back to that first Humane Society we visited as that woman said they were expecting a few more dogs for adoption to come in this afternoon."

Laura and Ellen enjoyed a delicious lunch of St. Louis style pork steaks with German potato salad and sautéed roasted root vegetables. They took their time and enjoyed a leisurely lunch with a nice glass of Rosé, then they ventured back to the Humane Society on Manchester near The Hill, a well-known and popular Italian community in the city.

They took their time and looked and visited with each new dog. But nothing was clicking with Ellen, she couldn't figure it out. She loved dogs. She loved Emma. Why wasn't she connecting.

"I don't know Laura," grimaced Ellen, "none of the dogs, I feel connect with me, nor I them.'

"Well sometimes it just takes time," suggested Laura, "but connecting is important. You need that bonding."

Just then as they sat in the little room that the Humane Society had set up for potential adopters to visit and get to know the dogs, the lady said they just got another dog from another humane society that reached its capacity and was full.

"Here she is," said the lady leading a Rottweiler into the little room where Ellen and Laura sat. The ladies were thrilled!

"Oh my god, she is like a little Emma," exclaimed Laura.

"Oh, Emma will love her!"

The volunteer shelter lady had led a bouncing young Rottweiler dog who looked just like Emma into the room. She appeared to be as sweet as Emma, too. And the dog was smart. Very smart. As if psychic and knowing which woman was looking for a dog, Little Emma walked right up to Ellen's thigh and buried her forehead right into Ellen, just like Emma does. And just as Emma did with Laura, when Laura first met her, in a way that said she wanted to go home with her.

"Okay, we'll take her," Ellen said without hesitation, "she's coming home with me." They were so excited and couldn't wait for Emma to meet the young Rottweiler, which Ellen named Mazy. And little Mazy, who the woman at the Humane Society thought was about two years old, seemed very happy to be going home with Ellen. Ellen was amazed that little Mazy was very smart and already well trained. Her owner had sadly passed from a sudden illness, and there was no one left to care for her, but now little Mazy had a new home.

Chapter Forty-Eight

The ladies stopped by Pet Smart at Brentwood Square with Mazy to let her pick out her own doggie bed, a few toys, and some treats. Mazy seemed so happy, as were the ladies. The ladies could not wait to get home with Mazy so she could meet Emma. They were so excited and looking forward to walking both dogs in the park.

Laura and Ellen were not a bit surprised to see Emma and Mazy connect and get along so well. One morning soon after, when Ellen was over at Laura's watching the dogs get better acquainted, the ladies could tell Mazy would likely learn a lot from older and well-trained Emma. The ladies sat on the couch chatting while the dogs played and did not notice when things began to get quiet behind them. They turned around and looked to see what the dogs were up to. They were surprised when they turned around to see what the two dogs were doing.

"Oh, must be time for a walk," laughed Laura as she

saw Emma sitting there with her leash in her mouth. They burst into tearful giggles when they saw little Mazy sitting next to Emma with her leash in her mouth, too. The hook was positioned low enough for Emma to reach and retrieve her leash and Laura had put a hook there for little Mazy too. It was clear to see they were great buds already as both patiently waited for the ladies to get a move on. It was time for a walk in the park.

It was such a pretty day. The ladies decided to walk a bit around their neighborhood over to Wydown Avenue, then cross Skinker Boulevard at the traffic light and enter the park there. They walked the sidewalk, Mazy did very well. She was watching and learning from Emma.

As the ladies walked on a bit near the lake, they noticed that traffic was stopped. As they got closer, they saw what all the commotion was about, seems mama duck was leading a parade of baby ducks across the street up the curb toward the lake. But three little ducks at the tail end of the little parade were too small still and struggled to get up the curb. Of course, mama duck never turned around to see if all the little ducklings were following. If she would have turned around she would have seen that the other slightly bigger ducks made it up the curb just fine, but the last three little baby ducks were on their own now and trying to scramble up the curb.

The three little ducks struggled with all their might to get up the curb. It was painful for the ladies to watch. But then Emma took charge and quietly, slowly, walked over to the little ducks struggling to get up the curb. They did not appear to be afraid of Emma, as if they sensed she only wanted to help them. Using her nose Emma gently gave one little duck a boost up the curb and that little baby duck quickly ran over to join mama and the rest of the ducks getting into the water at the lake. Two more little ducks were struggling. As if they knew what to expect, the little ducks slowed their struggling when they realized Emma was going to help.

Emma gently gave the little duck a boost up with her nose as the ladies watched in loving awe and admiration. And then little Mazy wanted in on the action. She had watched Emma. She was a quick learner, and as Emma boost the second little duck up, Mazy gently boosted the third little duck up the curb and it too ran over to join mama duck and the rest of the flock. Both dogs and the two ladies, as well as all the people stopped in their cars smiled and cheered, some had taken pictures. Emma and Mazy heard the commotion behind them from the cars and they proudly sat down side-by-side, little Mazy watching Emma. They did their good deed for the day, and they felt very proud.

"Such good girls you both are," Laura praised, feeling very proud and bending slightly to pat Emma's head and give her a hug., Ellen lovingly praised Mazy.

"Come on girls, lets continue on with our walk in the park," Ellen said after the dogs finished with their treat rewards for their good deed they walked on.

"I think we have come full circle, Ellen," smiled Laura, "Isn't this where we met last year when you and I helped that little duck get up the curb?

"Yes, you were the hero that day," sighed Laura, "I merely ran the little duck out into the street traffic."

"You did, I remember that," Ellen said giving Laura a quick hug.

"You were the hero that day, you saved that little duck."

"Oh Laura, it was just a walk in the park You are my hero, you offered me shelter, loaned me money, freed me from bondage in the basement, remember that, and even with bullets whizzing by your head," smiled Ellen with tears in her eyes, "you are my hero."

"It was my pleasure, what are friends for, right?

"I can't tell you how wonderful I feel being free of that horrible man," sighed Ellen.

"There are nice men in the world, like my husband Hank was. You'll meet a nice man one day."

"Don't think I am in any hurry, now that I am for the first time in my life independent and free to make my own decisions and choices. I am happy just as things are. I started an online abusive woman's help group. And now I might even write that book I thought about writing."

"Oh, way cool," Laura said.

"Hey how about the Boathouse for lunch?" offered Ellen. "My treat."

Of course, then both dogs looked up at Ellen, since they heard their favorite word, "treat." So now they were expecting just that, a treat. Both ladies obliged their beloved pups.

And so, peace had finally come to Ellen, with Laura's help. The dark cloud that hung over Ellen's head was finally gone. She could breathe again.

"I love being outdoors on such a beautiful spring day," smiled Laura, "don't you."

"Yep, just a walk in the park," agreed Ellen.

About the Author

This is Dianne Zimmermann's sixth novel. Her other books are *Just a Thought Away, Emma's Run, Jane's Aliens, Hooch Runners, Pleasant View* and *Three Days and a Gallon of Rose* were published by BookCrafters. Dianne lives in St. Louis and enjoys writing, drawing, photography, running, hiking and road trips.